Stars Align
KC De la Rosa

Contents

Dedication

For all the burnt out artists who thought they'd never be able to create again. I was you, and so was Clement. You can do it. I believe in you.

Glossary of Terms

Alqen (al-ken) - A planet in the Kratos galaxy. Its surface is made of aetherite, a mineral that looks like crystal. Its atmosphere is very cold. Qintaril originate from Alqen.

Daocury (dow-cure-ee) - A planet in the Kratos galaxy. Its surface is hard and rocky, and its atmosphere is very hot. Drask originate from Daocury.

Drask - An alien species originating from Daocury. They are typically dragon-like in nature, with two heads and scales of differing colors.

Drucaro (drew-car-oh) - An alien species originating from many different planets in the Kratos galaxy. They have four arms and are generally tall, six feet tall or more.

Kratos Galaxy - The next galaxy over from the Milky Way, Kratos consists of fifteen planets and their moons.

Orlix (or-licks) - An alien species originating from many different planets in the Kratos galaxy. They are characterized by their pointed ears, small horns that curve up from their foreheads, and long, thin vines of darkly pigmented skin that line their arms and legs.

Qintaril (kin-tah-rill) - An alien species originating from Alqen. They are generally tall, with the average qintaril standing over 6'5". They are characterized by the keratinous horns that curve around their heads and the keratinous plates of tissue that cover the tops of their arms and legs. Their skin is generally in shades of grays and blues.

Ta'qel (tah-kel) – Qin word, term for 'spouse.'

Veterok-III - The planet that Stars Align takes place on. It is considered a hub for activity in Kratos, and is more modern in its style. The climate is varied, with its Southern hemisphere being warmer than the Northern.

Dear Reader

Welcome to Stars Align! I'm so excited to have you here! I hope you love Qaed and Clement just as much as I do. These boys truly mean the world to me.

I have a couple of notes to prepare you for reading!

Firstly, a side character, Vendi, who you might remember from Starcrossed, uses he/she pronouns.

Second, Stars Align is a sweet rom com first and foremost, but it does have its share of serious moments and topics. So as a warning, this book contains:

Parental death, off page and mentioned
Alcohol abuse (in past, but discussed at length)
Brief depiction of disordered eating from a side character

As always, please take care of yourself when reading.

Kingsley

Vandu steeled her jaw, lifting her chin. "My name is Straal," she said easily, just as she'd practiced. She spoke from the base of her throat, though it didn't make her voice as deep as intended. "Ilit Straal, reporting for duty, sir."

The captain standing before her quirked an eyebrow, and for a moment, she worried that her cover had been blown with a mere two sentences. He appraised her with two sets of black eyes, a frown settling into his lips. "Ilit. You are smaller than your application stated," he said, smoothing a hand over his short-cropped black hair. He blew a scoff from his nostrils, thrusting a gray uniform into Vandu's hands. "Welcome aboard. Step aside, and we will show you to your barracks."

This was it. This was where it all began.

– Excerpt from *To Spite a Raven's Heart* by Clement Hall

Chapter One

Clement

"OOH, YOU SHOULD GET a bedazzled one, Clem. Then we can match!"

Clement had tuned out Candy's voice a while ago–mainly for the sake of his own sanity. He loved her to pieces, but he wasn't sure he'd ever felt so overwhelmed in his twenty-nine years of life. The shop they were in to get Clement's comm set up was not unlike an Apple Store on Earth; entirely too big, with oppressive white lighting that Clement had to squint against and employees that Clement found himself trying to avoid. After four days of being crammed in Candy's shuttle between Earth and Veterok-III, he was a little too tired for this.

"I don't need anything bedazzled," he grumbled, raking his fingers through his hair. A purple-skinned alien with two sets of black eyes and an equal amount of arms typed soundlessly on a holographic keyboard, their eyes fixed on the screen in front of them as they set up Clement's comm.

"Well, come look at these, then!" Candy peered into the glass countertop, where rows of comm wrist bands laid out in front of her. There were a lot of bedazzled wrist bands, including one set with pink stones like the one that shimmered on Candy's wrist. It suited her. Everything did. But Clement was pretty sure he couldn't pull it off.

"How tall are you?" came the cashier's voice, their eyes not moving from their screen.

"Uh, 5'9"."

He was met with a wordless blink. Right. America was the only country that didn't use the metric system–the likelihood of this random planet in the middle of an entirely different solar system using it was slim.

"Shit, what's that in centimeters?"

"153 centimeters," Candy said after a quick search on her own comm. He had to admit, they were kind of cool. The search would've probably taken a lot longer on his cell phone.

Speaking of which. "Oh, and can you give me a chip for my cell phone so I can talk to my sister back on Earth?" he asked, brandishing his slightly battered cell phone to the cashier.

"Sure." They typed some more, and Clement's eyes landed on the name tag pinned to their chest. *Grami*. His name felt particularly ordinary in comparison. "Weight?"

Clement squirmed. "Do you really need that information?"

"It's just for if your comm gets lost," the cashier said. "We need your identifying information so we can get it back to you."

"Two hundred forty-five," Clement said, glancing sideways at Candy. "Which is...."

"One hundred and eleven kilos." Candy gasped, pointing a blue manicured nail at another wrist band in the case. "Ooh, Clem, this one's cute, too. It's very you."

This time, she was actually right. The wrist band she pointed to looked like leather, but Clement was pretty sure leather didn't exist out here. The camel brown material was engraved with an ivy-like pattern–it would definitely match just about everything he owned.

"I do like that," he hummed, just as Grami asked for his address. Candy rattled it off for him, and it was only then that he realized he did have an address out here. In space. On a planet that he'd never been to before, never mind lived on.

A planet far away from everyone and everything he knew, except Candy. There was something liberating about being physically removed from the planet that held all of his problems, all of his stress. Also, his twin sister, but he didn't let himself dwell on that right now.

Grami asked about his wrist band and he pointed out the one Candy chose for him. After attaching a small electronic unit to it almost resembling a smart watch face, they passed it to him and picked his cell phone off the counter. "Just make sure it fits. I can adjust it if you need."

Clement rolled up the sleeve of his sweater and held his pale wrist out to Candy, who fastened the watch to it. It fit his thick wrist quite comfortably; the material was much softer than leather would have been, and was surprisingly breathable. "It's good, thanks."

A prompt for payment appeared from a small black box on the counter, and Candy tapped the face of her comm to it. Almost as quickly as Candy had paid, the cashier was handing Clement his phone back. "You should be able to make calls and send messages to Earth phones now," they said.

"Thank you so much, Grami," Candy chirped. She looped both of her arms around Clement's as they started for the exit. "You're official now, with your own comm and everything," she grinned. "What do you think?"

Truthfully, he still didn't know what he thought. The gravity of the situation hadn't quite sunk in yet—it didn't feel like he wasn't on Earth anymore. "I think... I'm freaking out a little."

"Ah, you'll get used to it," she said with a wave of her wrist. She gave his arm a squeeze, mashing her cheek into his shoulder. "Ugh, I'm so glad you're here."

Strangely enough, Clement was glad to be here, too. He was glad not to be at his house in Brooklyn, all of his free time spent rotting in bed because he couldn't figure out how to exist in the space anymore.

"I'm glad *you're* here," Clement said, stepping through the automatic door as it slid open with a hiss. The shop was in the middle of an outdoor shopping outlet, and while any other time he'd be delighted to look around, he really just needed a nap. His brain was so fried, he was surprised there wasn't smoke billowing from his ears. "So... to my new apartment, then?"

"Let's do it. I'm gonna shoot Qaed a message and let him know we're on our way."

Clement had never lived with a roommate before—at least, one that wasn't his twin sister. He wasn't sure how excited he was to have one, but at least he was paying a hell of a lot less in rent than he'd expected to. He was paying even less out here than he was back in Brooklyn.

Not that he was really worried about money. The one decent thing his mother had done before she died was leave him a tidy little nest egg, enough money to pay his rent for probably the next year and to fund his move out here in the first place. He wondered where she could've possibly gotten the money, but something told him going down that rabbit hole would do more harm than good.

Candy took him out to the bay, a parking lot-type area filled to the brim with vehicles. The shuttles out here varied in size and shape just as much as cars back on Earth; some plump and bulbous with long, awkward tails, some sleek and flat, almost sports car-like.

Candy's was more the latter; probably the size of a large pick up truck, with sharp, proud wings that jutted out of either side and a pointed snout that almost made it look reptilian. The exterior was a metallic midnight blue, and it felt very... Candy. She'd always liked shiny things.

"Damn, this dating app money's no joke, huh?" Clement joked as Candy gave him a boost into the shuttle. He relaxed a little as he realized how similar to a car it felt. The seatbelt was more like a harness that clasped between his legs, and the dashboard was much more intimidating than that of the Subaru he'd been driving since he was twenty.

Candy clambered into the driver's side, struggling a little more than Clement had. She secured the seatbelt over her ample chest, flipping all kinds of buttons and knobs on the dashboard. The shuttle rumbled to life beneath them, his seat vibrating with power.

"Yeah, dude. People were talking about Starcrossed for a hot minute because of the whole 'creators falling in love' thing, and it's just been uphill from there." Candy flashed a toothy grin in his direction. "You should download it. Get you an alien hottie to show you around."

Clement hadn't used a dating app in years. His mom got sick five years ago, and his social life became bedridden with her. When he wasn't at work, he was at home with her. He wasn't even sure he remembered how to date.

"Maybe. One thing at a time," he said, leaning back in his seat and turning to look out the window. The outlet mall disappeared behind them as they started for Clement's new apartment. It was jarring how fast Candy's shuttle was at first, but now that they were actually on planet, it wasn't so bad. He kind of liked watching the planet pass him by. There was so much of it he hadn't seen yet.

"Come on. Support a queer owned small business," Candy said, nudging him with her elbow.

"Fuck off." His attention shifted to Candy, who had reached over to squeeze his knee. Aside from his family, Candy was the person that had been in his life the longest. The Murdocks had moved next door to his family when Clement was a baby, back when his dad was still around. Candy's dad, ever the social butterfly, immediately brought three year old Candy over to meet Clement upon finding out that their new neighbors had twins Candy's age.

And the rest was history. She was there when Clement failed his first test and it felt like the end of the world, when he had his first kiss, when he had top surgery. When his mom got sick. Coming out to Kratos to be near her felt like the most natural thing to do.

"...Fine, I'll download it," Clement conceded. He fiddled with his comm for entirely too long, his pride not allowing him to ask Candy how to download an app. But he figured it out after navigating through entirely too many screens. "Number one in social apps across the hypernet?"

"Still. For six months, baby." Candy beamed.

Clement couldn't help but grin, too. Once the app downloaded, he flicked through the screens to set up a profile. He pored for entirely too long over his catalogue of selfies–the pickings were slim–and wasn't quite finished when they arrived at Clement's apartment.

Candy parked her shuttle on the ground level, but there had to be at least twenty levels of apartments and more rows than he could count. It was hard to tell where one apartment began and one ended. Each apartment was equipped with shuttle docks steps away from the front door, even the apartments on higher levels. He supposed that was the benefit of having vehicles that could fly.

The shuttle dock next to Qaed's apartment was empty, and Clement felt bad for being relieved. He just wanted to settle in without the pretense of having to meet someone else, especially the person that he was going to be living with for the foreseeable future.

Qaed's apartment was on the ground level, luckily, because Clement wasn't sure he'd be able to handle looking down from his front door at that height. Candy left him to lug his singular box of belongings out of the shuttle and tapped her comm to a data pad next to the door. The door answered with a click, and she pushed the door open.

The apartment was admittedly nicer than Clement had expected. The walls were very white and very clean, something Clement absolutely wasn't used to. The living room and kitchen were immediately visible from the front door, the living room sunken down a few steps and wrapped in an equally white, plush sectional sofa. A fireplace crackled against one wall of the living room, and upon closer inspection, Clement noticed that it was a very convincing holographic fire.

"Come on. I'll show you to your room," Candy said, leading Clement down a hallway with markedly empty walls. The place didn't even look lived in. The bedroom Candy led him to was no different; the walls were the same white as the living room, and the only furniture in it was a twin bed that had been stripped of its sheets and a dresser on the opposite wall.

Clement put his box down with a thump.

"Me and Votra used to fuck in here a lot," Candy grinned.

Suddenly, he didn't want to sleep in here anymore. "That is absolutely a fact that you could've kept to yourself."

"Could've. Didn't want to. The sex we had in here was good. The shower is surprisingly spacious, too."

Well now Clement wasn't going to be able to look Votra in the eye any time soon. "Yeah, yeah, you're in love and you get laid on a regular basis." He plopped down on the bed, the mattress squeaking under his weight. Where would he even go to get sheets?

"Don't worry, my little Clementine. You'll get there one day," Candy said, pinching his cheek. She sat on the bed next to him, looking at him with knowing eyes. "You gonna be okay?"

He would be. He always was. If there was one thing Clement Hall was good at, it was being okay when, all things considered, he really shouldn't be. "Yeah, I'm good. Promise." He placed a hand on the other side of her head and pulled her in to kiss the side of her head. "Thanks for everything. The comm and all that."

"'Course, babe. You know I got you." She stood, smoothing out her cheetah print dress. Only Candy Murdock could pull off such a garish print. "Oh, here." She held the screen of her comm towards Clement's, and it gave an affirmative ping. "Let me know if you need anything, okay? Don't pay for these shuttle taxis. They're a rip off."

And with that, Clement was left alone in his room. In his new apartment, on his new planet. His new galaxy.

And it made him feel so incredibly small. He shoved himself off the bed and rummaged through the single cardboard box that held everything he'd ever placed any importance on. It wasn't much–mostly clothes, some of the coffee equipment he'd collected over his almost ten years at Brewed Awakening. God, he was gonna miss coffee when he ran out.

And his laptop. The laptop that he hadn't touched in years–it'd be a miracle if it still worked. It still bore the stickers of his younger years; a chibi of a character from the anime he'd fixated on in his early twenties, a rat waving a trans flag. Clement's heart clenched. This time, when he opened his laptop, it would be different. He wouldn't have to smuggle in a handful of words between work and the demands of his home life. There wasn't a soul in this galaxy that expected a damn thing of him.

Actually, he wasn't sure how he felt about that. He gathered as much of his coffee gear into his arms as he could and brought it to the kitchen with only one goal in mind; christening his new apartment with a cup of coffee. He plugged in his gooseneck kettle to one of the adaptors Candy had given him, as well as his grinder, and filled the kettle with water before turning it on.

The familiar whirr of the kettle warming brought him a small amount of peace, a little bit of home in a place that felt, for lack of a better word, incredibly alien. The kitchen in particular was an enigma to him. He didn't recognize a single piece of equipment, save for what looked like an electric stovetop on the counter nearest the fridge.

Maybe he could have his new roommate explain everything to him. He snorted, popping a coffee filter into his Chemex with Sumatran coffee grounds that he was especially going to miss when they were gone.

He leaned against the counter, returning to Starcrossed as the kettle heated up. The profile setup was extensive but easy to follow, and he managed to finish setting up his profile just as the kettle clicked off.

It wouldn't hurt to swipe for a minute, right? He poured hot water over the grounds in a slow, calculated spiral as he read over the first profile the app presented to him. Ru'xo, an emerald skinned alien with tiny black horns and abs he wasn't afraid to show off, whose bio simply read 'Here for a good time, not a long time.'

"God, men out here are just as bad as on Earth," he said to himself, and immediately flicked his profile away.

Chapter Two

Qaed

"Okay, good job. Just a little more and I think you should stop for the day."

Qaed stood behind Jorai, spotting her as she returned the barbell to its stand. She laid back on the bench, her brick red bangs glued to her forehead with sweat. "Shit. How much weight was that?"

"A hundred and thirty kilos." Qaed stared at her pointedly. "You have gone up two weight sizes from yesterday."

"Hell yeah." She reached down to her side to take a swig from her water bottle. "Think I could go up one more?"

"Not without really hurting yourself." Jorai was actually going to be the death of him. He loved her to death, but she was a meathead with more muscles than sense. At this point, he was training her out of obligation more than anything. If she were left to her own devices, she'd probably call him because she tore a ligament overexerting herself. "You will not be able to wrestle if you pull a muscle, you know."

"Okay, *Dad*." She set her water bottle back down and gripped the barbell with all four hands. Qaed steadied himself behind her, preparing to spot her when her tired muscles inevitably gave out.

His comm pinged with a message from Candy, and he glanced down for just long enough to read it.

> hiiiiii! just brought clem to ur place. u gonna be home soon?

Shit. He'd completely forgotten that Clement was coming today. He'd hardly been at his apartment in the last forty-eight hours–between his time at the gym and the bar, he'd only come home to sleep and shower before going out again.

> Sorry, I am at the gym. But I will be there in an hour or two.

"Everything good?" Jorai grunted, her muscles starting to wobble with overexertion. Qaed rested his hands on the barbell, preparing himself to take the full weight if he needed to.

"Clement is already at my apartment." Qaed said, pulling up on the weight a little as Jorai lifted.

"Oh, shit. I forgot Clement was moving in with you." Jorai grunted, letting out a labored puff of air.

Truth be told, Qaed wasn't overly concerned about whether he had a roommate or not. Even when he lived with his sister, he didn't see her often. He was out of the house more often than not, and having a new roommate wasn't likely to change that.

"Yeah?" Qaed helped Jorai return the barbell to its stand, and Jorai pushed herself to a sitting position. He reached down for her water bottle and passed it to her. "I do not know if that is a good sign or a bad one."

"She said he's pretty quiet. So maybe you'll be the one to drive him crazy." Jorai flashed her fanged grin at him. "You should go meet him. I'll finish up here."

Qaed folded his arms over his chest. "I am not leaving you here alone until you are in the locker room." During his time as a bounty hunter, he'd met more than his share of Jorai's type. The ones who would work out until their bodies gave out on them and hardly ate enough to make up for the calories they were burning. If they weren't such close friends, she would have done his head in by now. "Have you eaten today?"

"Had a protein supplement this morning." Jorai shoved one of her hands into her black tank top and wiped her face with it.

Qaed clicked his tongue at her. "Eat a real lunch please. Do not make me call Xyxy."

Jorai rose to her feet, stretching her arms over her head. Qaed was pretty muscular himself, but Jorai made him look small. They were the same height, at 182 centimeters tall, but Jorai's muscles were nearly as wide around as Qaed's head. Drucaro were already predisposed to being large, and Jorai's relentless exercise habits only fed into that.

"Last time you did that, she made me sit out of my next match," Jorai huffed, raking her fingers through her tousled mullet.

"It is for your own good." He patted her square on the back. "Go take a shower. Now."

"You too. You fucking reek." Jorai grinned, swatting him with the sweat-soaked towel around her neck. "Thanks for today. I mean it, you should think about joining up with us full time."

He'd taken on the role of being Jorai's pseudo-training coach over the last few months, when being relegated to his apartment full-time started to make him stir crazy. Exhausting though she was, he liked the excuse to be out of the house. And it kept him in check, too; he usually squeezed in his own workout before meeting up with Jorai.

She and Xyxy, the manager of Jorai's wrestling promotion, had been begging him to train all of the other wrestlers. But Qaed wasn't sure he was ready for the responsibility. Training Jorai was hard enough.

Plus, taking on another official job meant that he had officially given up.

"I will think about it," Qaed said, his permanent response. He pointed a finger in her direction. "Eat lunch!"

Qaed could use some lunch himself. Maybe he should extend the offer to Clement.

He showered and dressed in a t-shirt and gray sweatpants before making his way home. It was weird to think that there would be someone else waiting for him when he got there. It had been six months since he'd come home to somebody.

And he wasn't sure how he felt about it. He tapped his comm against the data pad by the door and pushed the door open carefully so as not to startle him. A warm, bitter smell greeted him as he walked in, one that felt vaguely familiar. It almost smelled like the sour, mildly astringent coffee Votra had started making at home after meeting Candy, but better.

The scent led him to the kitchen, where the human who had to be Clement leaned against the counter, comm screen projected in front of him. He'd recognize the interface of Starcrossed anywhere. He had an account that he could never quite bring himself to use. Something about using an app his sister developed for hooking up felt fundamentally wrong.

He didn't have a lot of experience with humans, outside of Candy. Women, tragically, weren't his type. But Clement was a different story. He wore a chunky knit cream sweater with the sleeves rolled up to his elbows, revealing pale-skinned arms coated in thick brown hair. The hair atop his head was the same color, shaggy, falling about his round face. Two squares of glass sat in front of his eyes, framed by silver metal. Much of his figure was obscured by the baggy sweater, and Qaed found himself wondering what he would look like without it on.

At least introduce yourself before you start mentally taking his clothes off, he told himself, padding into the kitchen. "Hey, I know that guy," Qaed said. "I would not recommend matching with him. He can be kind of... abrasive."

Clement startled, fumbling with his comm screen as he struggled to turn it off. "W-Wh–Hey, you should announce yourself before just walking in here like that," he stammered, shoving his comm hand behind his back like he'd been caught doing something bad. His cheeks were stained pink, his plush lips parted with irritation.

Gods, he was even more beautiful up close. He didn't know whether he was pissed at Candy for inviting him here or if he wanted to shower her with praise. "I thought you had heard me walk in. The door lock is not exactly quiet."

"I was... occupied." Clement turned his attention to a strangely shaped glass apparatus that seemed to be the source of the delicious smell. "You know this guy?"

"Unfortunately." Qaed's encounters with Emei were the unfortunate product of a few *very* drunk nights–Qaed found himself stumbling into Emei's four strong, green arms more often than he should. "How many unsolicited dick pics have you gotten?"

Clement paled. "Actually, none. He just... asked me for one."

"You are lucky you did not just *get* a picture of his dick. It *is* a nice one, but a little frightening when you are not expecting it." Qaed leaned against the counter next to Clement, watching as he poured water on top of what looked like mud. *Humans are weird.*

"Great. Good to know I dodged a bullet." Clement put the kettle down. "I totally thought men out here would be better than the men on Earth."

"Men are terrible, no matter where you go," Qaed chuckled. "I could set you up on a date if you would like."

Clement scoffed. "No thanks. The first thing Candy told me about you was *not* to let you set me up on a date."

Qaed pressed a hand to his chest in feigned shock. "I will have you know that I have a generally positive track record for setting my friends up on dates. Candy was an unfortunate outlier." He moved to Clement's side, peering into the glass device. "What are you doing?"

"Making coffee." Clement edged away from Qaed slightly, narrowing his deep brown eyes. Qaed had always thought humans had beautiful eyes–even Candy's captivated him sometimes. "Do you want some?"

So it *was* coffee. He'd decided a while back that he didn't particularly enjoy it without heaps of sugar, but he couldn't have Clement thinking he was uncultured. "Sure. Thank you." He leaned his hip against the counter, watching Clement with amusement as he rummaged through the cabinets for mugs. The hem of his shirt lifted as he reached, revealing a sliver of skin along the waistband of his jeans.

He averted his gaze, clearing his throat. "Um, next cabinet."

"You could've led with that."

Qaed didn't look back at Clement until he heard the clink of porcelain mugs against the counter top. Clement discarded the paper cone and divided the hot brown liquid between two mugs. "Sorry, I only made enough for one cup."

"Well, I appreciate you sharing it with me," Qaed said, watching as Clement raised the mug to his lips. There was a dusting of dark hair across Clement's upper lip to match the patch of it at his chin. "And it is nice to officially meet you. I apologize again for frightening you."

Clement gave a little half-hearted laugh. "It's fine." He cast a pointed look at Qaed's mug. "You like the coffee?"

Qaed took a sip and immediately, bitterness burst across his tongue, giving way to something he didn't entirely recognize. It was almost... sweet, creamy. A "whoa" slipped out of him. This was nothing like what Votra and Candy used to make.

Clement grinned. "It's a good one. Honduran. Not that... you know where that is. Sorry, I'll spare you all of the nerdy coffee talk."

"Thank the gods. I was going to play it off like I had any idea what you were talking about."

"That would've been embarrassing for you. I would've noticed immediately." Clement smiled again with all his teeth, and it was only then that Qaed noticed the gap in between the front two. *Cute.*

"Good thing I did not try." Qaed took another sip of coffee and placed his mug on the counter. "I hope that you have gotten settled in alright. Sorry I was not here to greet you when you got here."

Clement dismissed Qaed's concern with a wave of his hand. "It's all good. I didn't bring much, and Candy kind of helped."

"*Candy* helped you carry in your things?"

"Well... no. She was just there for moral support." Clement laughed, shielding his mouth with his hand. Even his laugh was adorable.

"Sounds about right." Qaed drained the last of his coffee, dutifully placing his mug in the small countertop sanitizer. Clement's mouth fell open a fraction once the mug emerged, steaming hot and spotlessly clean. "I am sure you are exhausted after your days of traveling."

Clement opened the tray of the sanitizer and put his own mug in it, fumbling with the controls for a second before Qaed reached over to turn it on for him. "Whoa," he breathed, watching the machine as it whirred. "Uh, actually, I'm feeling pretty good. I think my brain is so overwhelmed, sleep is the last thing on it, y'know?"

"Makes sense." Qaed watched as Clement took the clean mug into his hands; he'd always thought human hands seemed so impractical, with their tiny, longer fingers and impossibly small palms. Clement's were pretty, the tops of them dusted with a thin coat of the same hair that coated his arms. "Well, to commemorate our first night as roommates... would you like to go out for dinner?"

Clement's lips formed an 'o.' "Sure, I'd love that." He gave Qaed a bashful smile that made him weaker in the knees than he'd like to admit.

"I only have one request."

Clement tilted his head. "Okay."

"You have to let me look at your Starcrossed matches. You do not know what this planet has in store for you, and I feel it is my duty as your roommate to protect you."

Clement laughed again, placing his mug in the cabinet. "Okay, deal."

The barracks were bare, save for the two cots shoved up against either corner of the room. At least she'd have the luxury of not sharing a room with every other hunter in the facility. She peeled her gray uniform top off, her skin screaming with relief. The material itched, and she was only just convinced she wasn't allergic to it.

Her door opened with a resounding slam, and she let out a squeal that she immediately covered with a harsh cough. "Damn, would it kill you to knock?" she ground out, shoving her arms back into her sleeves very much against her will.

"On the door of my own room?" came an amused voice from behind her. "Sorry, mate. You want me to take my shoes off when I enter, too?" The door closed with a click, and Vandu turned on her heel with every intention of firing back.

But instead, she came face-to-face–or rather, face-to-chest–with a smirking drucaro, one set of hands on his hips. His inky black curls were free from their mandated bun, framing his infuriatingly handsome face. When he smiled, all four of his eyes curved into crescents.

"Straal, right? Dholzi." He bowed his head in greeting–a very shallow *bow, Vandu noticed. "Sorry to interrupt your changing. Feel free to continue. Pretend I'm not here."*
Something told Vandu that would be terribly *hard to do.*

– Excerpt from To Spite a Raven's Heart by Clement Hall

Chapter Three

Clement

CLEMENT ACTUALLY COULDN'T REMEMBER the last time he'd gone out for dinner.

The entire flight over in Qaed's shuttle–which was quite nice, he noticed–he found himself giddy with excitement. If he didn't count the out-of-date food he smuggled from the coffee shop, he'd cooked all of his own meals over the last few years. With his mother's hyper-specific diet and Cecily's even more hyper-specific safe foods, he couldn't even risk picking up buttered noodles from the Italian place down the street.

The excitement flopping like a fish in the pit of his stomach only grew when they parked in a shuttle bay a short ride from the apartment. Qaed had given him a short run-down about the planet on the ride over; rather than being divided into towns and countries like Earth was, it was divided into districts. Some were the size of neighborhoods, others the size of cities.

The district Qaed took them to was the former. It almost felt like an outlet mall; the shuttle bay was directly in the center, and they were surrounded by department stores, restaurants, spas, and offices. A shuttle parked not far from them whirred to life as Clement stepped out of Qaed's, and Clement's hair whipped about his face as it took off.

He really wasn't on Earth anymore. He stuffed his hands in his pockets, glancing towards Qaed. He'd changed clothes before leaving the house; he wore a simple sleeveless black turtleneck and a pair of baggy black pants that hung dangerously low on his sharp hips. Every time Qaed moved, the hem of his shirt rode up, revealing the dark gray muscles beneath them.

Clement cleared his throat as if to clear away the inappropriate thoughts that crept into his head. "So, where are we going?" he asked, following at Qaed's heels as he started to walk.

"Cafe Strelka," Qaed said. "I thought you might appreciate somewhere a bit more quiet."

Clement felt his cheeks grow warm. "...I would. Thank you."

The cafe was nestled between two smaller shops in a less busy area of the district. It reminded Clement of the smaller mom and pop cafes back home—unassuming from the front, with a small metal nameplate against the brick that read 'Cafe Strelka,' an ornate arrow etched beneath it. Qaed held the door for Clement, and Clement thanked him with a shy smile.

The walls inside were clearly steel painted a streaked brown that was meant to resemble wood, and it kind of worked. Paintings of varying sizes dotted the walls, drawing attention away from the shoddy paint job; there were portraits of aliens of all species, of plants, of buildings Qaed and Clement had passed on their way over. Clement felt warmer just being inside, despite the fact that the wall facing out into the district was drawn open, letting in the evening draft.

This was exactly what Clement needed. His stomach growled as it registered the scent in the air, a scent that he didn't recognize but was unmistakably food. Qaed stared at him. "Are you alright?" he asked warily.

Clement placed a hand to his stomach, suddenly self conscious. "Humans' stomachs make noises when we're hungry. I know, it's weird."

"Yeah, it is." Qaed grinned and Clement elbowed him, following him through the restaurant. A droid the size of a large dog directed them to a table; he remembered Candy's texts about the bowtied robots a few months ago, but he didn't think he'd be lucky enough to see them on his first night on the planet.

The droid deposited them at a booth with high-backed benches. The cushion beneath him was almost too soft, his body sinking into it like quicksand. Getting up was going to be a struggle, but he'd worry about that later.

Qaed slid into the booth opposite him, taking the menu in both hands. "They have very typical Veterok-III food here. Very comforting, but very fried," he said, flipping immediately to the back of the menu.

Clement followed suit. The cocktail menu was intimidating; he hadn't heard of half the things on the menu, but he couldn't remember the last time he'd had a drink. Hell, it was his first night in a new galaxy, in his new home. In this place that frankly scared the shit out of him. He was going to have a drink or two.

Their waiter, a teal-skinned orlix with fluffy curls that sat about her head like a cloud, approached to take their order only a few minutes later. Qaed ordered a drink that Clement wasn't sure he'd be able to pronounce, and just as Clement was about to order the same, Qaed said, "And a *coquim* for him, please." Well, that was hotter than it had any right being.

"So, tell me about yourself, Clement," Qaed said, and Clement lifted his head.

Tell me about yourself. He mulled the question over in his mind for what must have been a beat too long. "Shit, sorry. I did not mean to ask you the hard-hitting questions right away," Qaed said, his tone teasing. He laced his fingers together and rested his chin on them, holding Clement's gaze so intently his first instinct was to look away.

Make friends, Clement, he told himself. *Especially with your roommate.* The last thing he needed in a brand new galaxy was a roommate that he awkwardly skirted around whenever he was home. "I just haven't been asked that in a while," he said, picking at one of his fingernails. "Uh, I'm twenty-nine. I have a twin sister named Cecily, who still lives on Earth. I'm...." A barista? A writer? The latter was laughable–he hadn't put a word to paper in years. And referring to himself as a barista in a galaxy that didn't even *have* coffee felt silly.

The server spared him, delivering their drinks. Qaed's looked simply like a glass of soda water with a wedge of some sort of pink citrus sitting on the rim. Clement's was in a shorter glass; an amber colored liquor with what looked like a perfectly cubical stone in the center. "What's that?" Clement asked, picking up the glass and staring into it. That was *definitely* a rock.

"Lorgosite. It is for keeping the drink cold," Qaed said, taking a sip.

Clement did the same, half expecting the oaky punch of bourbon to hit him. But it didn't. Instead, a sharp, almost citrus-y taste tingled at the edges of his tongue, making his mouth water. A spiced warmth that reminded him of ginger followed it, settling across his taste buds.

"Holy shit, that's good," Clement laughed incredulously. "Remind me to take your recommendations more often."

"Trust me, I will. I have *excellent* taste in food and beverage."

Clement's brows crept up. "Oh, and you're so humble, too. Is there anything you can't do?"

Qaed laughed again, and Clement couldn't help but think he wasn't *that* funny. "No. No, there is not." He lifted his glass to his lips. "So, you were saying?"

Damn. He'd hoped Qaed would move on. Clement was honest to a fault–he wouldn't be able to lie to Qaed if he tried. "I was gonna tell you what I am, but I guess I don't really know. I was a barista back on Earth, but I can't really do that out here since you don't have coffee."

"Well, what do you *want* to do out here?" Qaed's eyes didn't move from Clement, making Clement feel a bit like a bug under a microscope.

He took a longer sip of his drink this time. It made the edges of his nerves tingle in a way that made talking about himself just a little less terrifying. "I... guess I wanna write. I didn't really have the time to do it back home, but now I have all the time in the world."

"What kind of things did you write?" Qaed asked.

Clement opened his mouth to speak, but the server approached to take their order. Qaed ordered something called *avocet,* then turned to Clement. "Do you know what you would like?"

Clement was normally the *study the menu before showing up* kind of guy, but it hadn't done him any good this time. "Not really," he said, raking his teeth over his lower lip.

"Would you like me to pick for you?"

He let out a sigh of relief. "If you don't mind."

Qaed ordered something for Clement, something Clement didn't remember seeing on the menu. But then again, he wasn't sure he would've committed it to memory if he'd seen it. He murmured a 'thank you' to Qaed as the server disappeared with their order.

"You are not going to get out of talking about yourself with these poorly timed server interactions," Qaed said with a bemused smile.

"Bold talk for someone who hasn't told me a word about himself all night," Clement shot back, folding his arms on the table and leaning forward. "What about you? What do *you* do?"

"Nothing right now. I am... what did Candy say? *Funemployed?*"

Clement snorted. "Well, I guess that makes both of us." That sounded like a recipe for not being able to pay their rent, but who was he to project his own insecurities onto Qaed? Clement had enough in his savings to cover his share of rent for well over a year, but he was already stressing about what he would do once it ran out.

"Sounds like we are going to be seeing a lot of each other, then." Something twinkled in Qaed's eyes that Clement couldn't place.

"I guess so. Which gives us *plenty* of time for you to unlock my tragic backstory. There's no fun in spilling it all tonight."

"Ah, so it *is* a tragic one? It seems you and I are not that different after all," Qaed said.

"Yeah?" Clement trailed a finger through the condensation gathering on his glass. "Maybe Candy and Votra were right to set us up as roommates, then."

"I think you are right. I suppose there is a reason that they are the ones who made the dating app and not us." Qaed paused. "I mean... in the way that they are good at pairing people together. Not exclusively in the dating sense."

Clement's hands flew to his pinkening cheeks. "Right, yeah. Of course."

A silence fell over them that wasn't entirely uncomfortable. But Clement was definitely in over his head. Qaed was right, they *weren't* dating, but if they were, Qaed would be miles out of his league. *Light years.*

Their food came out a few quiet minutes later, and Clement's stomach growled in response to the introduction of delicious new smells. Balls of something fried sat atop a bed of a heavily spiced orange-brown sauce, sprinkled with some sort of green herb.

Clement dug his fork into one of the balls, and it crumbled with very little effort. The ball was filled with a mixture of some kind of pearled grain and chunks of vegetable, and when he took a bite, an explosion of spices filled his mouth. The bite was rich and flavorful, and he couldn't stop himself from taking another bite immediately.

"So? Ratings? Reviews?" Qaed asked, wiping a smear of sauce from the corner of his mouth with his thumb.

Ripping his gaze from Qaed's lips, Clement wiped his mouth with a napkin. "Hmm. While I am no expert in the world of Veterok-III's native cuisine, my palate *is* quite refined." Clement puffed out his chest. "It's spiced but not *too* spiced. Rich, heavy, but not in an unpleasant way. I found myself wanting to keep eating, despite the spice making my nose run. I would give it... four and a half out of five stars."

"Stars? Why stars specifically?" Qaed asked, poking his fork into one of the balls.

Clement exhaled a laugh through his nose. He hadn't considered just how different such mundane things would be out here–what was the Veterok-III version of Google reviews? "I dunno, actually. That's just what we've always used on Earth. Now that you mention it... ranking something out of *five* is kinda weird."

"So what would make it five stars?"

Clement pursed his lips. "Some acid, maybe? To cut through all the fried-ness?"

"Hmm. That is fair." Qaed pointed his fork at Clement. "I think you could get a job as a food critic out here. I am sure many of our galaxy's citizens would love to hear critiques of our food from the eyes of a human."

Clement's eyes narrowed. "That sounded sarcastic."

"Did it?" He winked, and Clement's food turned to stone in his stomach. Why couldn't Candy have warned him that she'd set him up with a roommate that was *exactly* his type? He'd laughed more in the last few hours than he had in the last month, and Qaed's easy smile did something to his nerves. Not to mention the sharp jaw, prominent cheekbones, the broad chest that tapered into a slender waist that begged to have Clement's hands on it–

Clement choked, thumping his chest with a fist. *That was karma. Get your head out of the gutter.*

"Are you alright?" Qaed asked.

"Yep. Just, uh, went down the wrong pipe."

Qaed blinked a few times. "Gods, how have you humans survived this long?"

Clement often found himself wondering the same thing. "Spite, I think." He downed the last of his drink in the attempt at clearing his throat, but the spice did little to quell the situation.

But the rest of the dinner went by accident-free. Clement didn't choke again, no matter how distracting he continued to find Qaed. If anything, conversation with Qaed became easier. He still didn't talk about himself much, save for telling him the story of how he'd become Jorai's personal trainer. "When the person who shoved you into a taxi at your drunkest tells you they need a personal trainer, it is difficult to say no," Qaed was saying as a waiter that wasn't theirs approached him. Clement's eyebrows raised curiously as the server leaned down to murmur something to Qaed. Qaed's brow furrowed and whispered something back, but the server nodded and disappeared before he finished speaking.

"What was *that* all about?" Clement asked.

"It appears that she has us confused for someone else," Qaed said, "and I tried to tell her that, but she did not listen. So now she is bringing us a free dessert under the pretext that I am proposing to you."

It was a good thing Clement wasn't still eating, or else he would have *definitely* choked again. "W-What?"

Qaed shrugged a shoulder as if this were a common occurrence. "Unless you wanted to do the proposing. I would be alright with that."

"Qaed, we can't pretend to get engaged in front of all these people for a *free dessert*. That's–" He floundered. He remembered a time or two in his childhood that his mother had said it was Clement's birthday when it wasn't, all for the sake of a free piece of cake. It'd felt wrong back then, too. "That's, like, stealing!"

"Hardly. They are *giving* it to us, remember?"

Clement gaped so widely, he felt like his jaw might unhinge. The server returned with a tart piled high with fluffy cream and placed it in front of Qaed with a knowing wink. Well, it was a good thing Clement wasn't *actually* being proposed to, because this was far from subtle.

"I can't believe you're doing all this for a *free dessert*," Clement groaned, his eyes following Qaed as he stood. He was *really* doing this.

Qaed rounded the table and rested a hand on the back of Clement's side of the booth, leaning in close to him. His cool breath ghosted the shell of Clement's ear, sending a violent shiver down his spine. "Think of it as a gift for you. As a welcome to the planet," he said, then lowered himself to his knees on the floor by Clement's feet.

All Clement could think about was the fact that Qaed could have just *bought* him a dessert as he took Clement's hand in both of his. "My dearest Clement... I hope that I can find the right words to convey what I am trying to say to you tonight, in front of all of the patrons of this restaurant."

All of the patrons was right. There were more sets of eyes on them than Clement knew how to handle. He wanted to yank Qaed up off his knees, but God, did he look good on them. His giant, oil-slick eyes stared into Clement's, and he felt like he could disappear into them.

"I may not have the money for the beautiful jewelry you deserve, but the one thing I do not lack is love in my heart for you," Qaed said in earnest, and Clement fought the urge to giggle. "I hope you will forgive me for the timing not being the best–" Well, he was right about that. "--But will you do me the greatest honor of being mine for the rest of time?"

Maybe it was the alcohol, or the fact that no one had held his hand for this long in years, but Qaed's words brought tears to his eyes. He sniffled, wiping his lashes with the heel of his palm. "Yes, Qaed, of course I will."

The restaurant erupted into cheers around them and Qaed rose, leaning over to pull Clement into a hug. "Excellent acting, Clement," he whispered.

Yeah, of course. He was just *such* a good actor. The thought of someone loving him this much was *definitely* not what made him cry. "You too," he said with a watery laugh. Qaed returned to his seat and Clement ducked his head, doing his best to rid his face of the evidence of his tears.

Qaed dug into the dessert first, pulling back a spoonful of fluffy white cream. "Go on. Try it," he said.

So he did. And maybe it was worth the embarrassment. The tart was all cream and what had to be a fruit; the creamy pulp was custard-like, with a tang not unlike a slightly underripe strawberry. A knowing smile touched Qaed's lips. "Not so mad at me anymore, are you?"

"I guess I can get over it. But next time, if you can't afford dessert, you can just tell me," Clement said teasingly.

Their server arrived with to go boxes and the news that another table had paid their tab. She directed their attention to a table only a few away from theirs, where an elderly qintaril and a human Clement had to assume was their partner waved at them. Clement clamped a hand over his mouth.

"Oh my God. Are we assholes?" he whispered.

"I certainly feel much worse now," Qaed said back. "We have to get out of here."

"Agreed." Clement shoveled another mouthful of dessert into his mouth before standing. Qaed leaped out of his seat and all but shoved Clement out of the restaurant, artfully avoiding the elderly couple.

The moment the cool evening air greeted them, they both erupted into giggles. "Way to go, Qaed. You just stole money from old people!" Clement managed between bouts of laughter.

"How was I supposed to know that a particularly generous old couple would be *that* happy for us?" Tears leaked from the corners of Qaed's eyes, and he brushed them away as he leaned against the side of the building. "Gods, we can never come back here again."

Clement's cheeks ached with the effort of his grinning, and strangely enough, he didn't want it to stop.

Vandu was exhausted. Training was much more intensive than she'd expected it to be, and it wasn't as if she hadn't been in shape before joining. She had to be. She had to pass for her bigger, bulkier brother, but things weren't looking good for her so far. She'd had curious eyes cast in her direction. Untrusting eyes.

She'd elected to skip going to the mess hall tonight. The less time she spent around scrutinizing eyes, the better. And maybe allowing herself to sit in her hunger would strengthen her resolve. The sooner she got through training, the sooner she could get out from under the captains' thumbs.

Vandu was on her second set of pushups when the door opened just enough to allow Dholzi to slip in. She didn't dare look up at him, especially once the tantalizing smell of warm spices and bread settled into the room. She felt particularly like this man was trying to torture her.

But instead, he crouched before her, thrusting a cloth-wrapped bundle under her nose. "Someone told me my roomie was starving himself out in here," he said. "You know that, once your body runs out of nutrients, it just starts eating away at your muscles, right?"

Vandu wasn't strong enough to reject him. She moved to a sitting position with a grunt, and Dholzi sat cross-legged across from her. "How'd you get away with this?" she asked incredulously, unwrapping her bundle.

"Told 'em you were sick," he said with a shrug of his shoulders. "I tried to be real dramatic about it, too. I said I was camping out in the mess hall because you were fighting for your life in our room, so... make sure you play it up a little, okay?"

– Excerpt from *To Spite a Raven's Heart* by Clement Hall

Chapter Four

Clement

CLEMENT SPENT THE REST of his first week in his new galaxy acclimating–the best that he could, at least. He was still a little afraid to venture out of the apartment, but he'd made a less-than-accidental habit of coming out of his room when he heard Qaed come back in from working out in the morning. He was awake anyway; the barista hours hadn't quite worked their way out of his system yet.

And then, when Qaed went about his business, Clement sat down and wrote. He'd started the night after his dinner with Qaed and hadn't been able to stop. His writing was stilted and awkward; his voice hadn't quite returned to him. But it existed. And that was more than he could say about anything he'd attempted to do in the last few years.

On his eighth morning on Veterok-III, Qaed came home especially sweaty, and Clement's eyes locked on a bead of sweat trailing down the slope of his neck for entirely too long. He was trapped in a horny prison of his own making, and he needed to get out *desperately*. "Do you know if there are any book stores nearby?" he asked just as Qaed was about to go back to his room. Did they even *have* books out here?

"Probably in the Altai district," Qaed said, wiping his face with his shirt. "Would you like me to take you? I just need to shower and then I am free."

As much as Clement loved the idea of being trapped in a shuttle with Qaed, he was long overdue for a hangout with Candy. "It's okay. I'm gonna get Candy to pick me up," he said. "You want anything while I'm out?"

"I am alright, thank you." Qaed slipped his sweat-soaked tank top off and Clement forced his gaze to rest literally anywhere else. "Tell Candy I said hello."

"Will do," Clement said, trying not to let his eyes linger on Qaed's broad back as he headed down the hallway to his room. Yeah, he *definitely* needed to get out of here.

Luckily, Candy was in the shuttle bay within less than half an hour, and the bookstore was in the same district as Cafe Strelka. Being in a district that he recognized put him a little more at ease.

Candy looped her arm around Clement's as they walked into the bookstore, a very cozy shop dotted with soft puddles of chair that reminded Clement of the beanbag he'd had in his room as a kid. All he wanted to do was take a book from the shelves and sink into it for the rest of the day.

"*So*, what are you thinking of the planet so far?" Candy asked, immediately tugging Clement along as she made a beeline for the new releases. The shelves didn't look terribly different from the shelves of bookstores on Earth, save for the fact that every book was the exact same size and shape. Clement withdrew his arm from Candy as he pulled one off the shelf. It was much lighter than he expected, and when he opened it, rather than being greeted by paper pages, a screen came to life in front of him. He tapped through it like he did his eReader back at home. Earth *really* needed to catch up.

"I haven't gone out a ton, but I like it a lot so far," he said, slotting the book back into its place on the shelf. "It's kind of weird to be anywhere that isn't Brooklyn."

"I know, right?" Candy crouched, scanning the shelf next to Clement. "What about Qaed? How's living with him going?"

Clement's cheeks immediately warmed at the mention of Qaed, the vision of his bare, muscular back rushing back to the forefront of his mind. "Dude, you could've warned me that he's *stupid* hot."

"Oh my God, isn't he? The first time Votra introduced me to him, he kinda took my breath away." Candy took a book from the shelf, prompting a raise of Clement's eyebrows. He didn't know Candy read.

"Yeah, and he walks around the apartment *shirtless. A lot.*" Clement tapped through a book with a particularly beautiful cover, mainly to avoid looking at Candy.

Candy whistled. "Lucky you." If she weren't wearing such a dangerously short dress, he would have shoved her over. She rose from her squat with a grunt, and Clement took her hand to help her up. "You're welcome."

Clement definitely wasn't *complaining* about living with Qaed and being privy to his shirtlessness. But a little bit of time to adjust before he started flaunting his muscles would have been great.

He shifted over to an adjacent bookshelf to put some distance between himself and this conversation. Dwelling on how hot he thought Qaed was didn't benefit anyone. "I started writing again," he blurted out, as if this conversation would be any less mortifying.

Candy was one of very few people in his life that knew he was a writer. Though it wasn't a facet of his person that he was necessarily ashamed of, he'd received his fair share of criticism about what he chose to write. Candy, though, had never been one of those people. Her head jerked in his direction, her pink bob fluttering about her face. "Yay! Oh my God, that's so exciting!" She trotted over to him and threw her arm around his shoulders. "What are you writing?"

Maybe the fear of letting her down would brute force him into not quitting. "It's not much yet. Just some random little scenes that came to me," he said, peering at the steadily growing pile of books in Candy's arm. "You're gonna read all those?"

Candy trilled her lips. "Nope. These are for Votra. She asked me to pick them up for her while I was over here. This woman reads books like her life depends on it. And maybe one day she'll read yours."

He didn't know what he'd done to deserve Candy's unwavering confidence in him, but it felt misplaced. "Yeah, maybe." He wandered to the next row of shelves, which featured actual paperback books. He took one off the shelf and leafed through the pages, closing his eyes and breathing in the familiar smell of ink and paper. A wave of homesickness washed over him, and he clutched the book to his chest. Whatever book this was, it was coming home with him.

He'd sold his entire book collection years ago, tucked the three massive bookshelves' worth of books into cardboard boxes and sold them at the yard sale they'd held after his mom's first hospitalization. Maybe he'd sold his inspiration along with them.

Clement wandered to the front of the store, where Candy was purchasing her books and chatting up the cashier. He came to her side, and Candy plucked the book from his hands. "This is Clement, by the way," Candy said to the cashier, a pale blue-skinned alien with dark blue curls and two long antennae that poked through them from the top of her head. "Zanna here's a writer, too."

God, Clement should've just kept his mouth shut. "Hi," he said shyly as Candy put his book on the counter.

"Hi!" She slid the book across the countertop and a beep sounded from the monitor next to her. "You like Alitaya Strix?"

Truthfully, Clement hadn't paid attention to the book he'd picked up; it wasn't like he was familiar with Kratos-based authors anyway. "Uh, I've actually never read their books. This'll be my first."

"She's gonna be at the Yakut Writer's Conference at the end of the year," Zanna said, waving her small hand towards the payment terminal. Candy tapped her comm to it. "You should come! Her agent's gonna be at the pitch event, too."

Clement immediately felt like falling through the floor. Researching agents and making plans to attend pitch events had consumed his life at one point. He'd had spreadsheets and lists galore, budget plans, itineraries for the conferences he was going to attend. "Oh, I dunno," Clement grimaced. "I don't know if I'll have anything ready by then–"

"Maybe a deadline would be good for you," Candy said, bumping him with her hip. "The end of the year isn't so bad!"

"Yeah! Even if you don't pitch, you should still come. Especially if you're new to the planet. I didn't pitch last year, but I met a ton of other really cool writers," Zanna said. "Want me to send you the info?"

Everything in Clement told him he should go. He *knew* that he should. But the idea of it made him want to crawl out of his skin. He wasn't sure he loved the idea of being surrounded by *actual* writers, putting on the facade that he was one of them. "Sure," he said, and Zanna held her comm out to his. His comm buzzed on his wrist, the screen flashing with the received information.

"I sent you my comm info, too. Maybe we can meet up at the convention!" Zanna said, and she seemed so genuinely excited that Clement almost felt bad for considering not going.

It wasn't like he had anything else to do. He wasn't going to be working–or maybe he *should* be working by that point. His chest tightened and nerves tingled at his temples. Candy pressing his book into his hands was the only thing drawing him back to the present. "Thanks," he said finally, his tongue feeling especially heavy in his mouth.

He followed Candy out of the bookstore, feeling a little less overwhelmed once he filled his lungs with fresh air. "Wow, a week on Veterok-III and you're already going to a writing conference!" Candy said, slinging her tote bag full of books over her shoulder.

"Hey, I never said I was going," Clement said, leaning against the brick wall of the store. He finally looked down at the book in his hands; Veilbound by Alitaya Strix. It was safe to assume it was a fantasy sort of romance, the cover decorated with intricate vines snaking around a rusted sword. Book trends didn't stop within the Milky Way, it seemed.

"But why wouldn't you?" Candy folded her arms over her chest, giving him that look she always did. The look that meant she was sparing his feelings by not speaking her mind in that exact moment.

"Because I'm not a writer, Candy." He didn't look away from the book. He thumbed through the pages for a moment until Candy stuck her hand into it, stopping him.

"What *is* a writer, then?" she asked indignantly. "Do you remember that time in middle school when I told you I wanted to read a story about a hot lady night rescuing a hot lady princess?"

Clement huffed out a small laugh through his nose. "I do remember that." He'd pored over his spiral bound notebook until the wee hours of the morning for months perfecting that story.

"Do you remember that *other* time in ninth grade when Mrs. Shelton told the entire class that she wouldn't be surprised to see you published one day?"

Clement had always thought she was saying that to be nice. He shrugged a shoulder. "I mean–"

"And what about the time you won that award in second grade for that poem you wrote?"

"Okay, to be totally fair, I think I was one of the only kids that actually *tried–*"

"Dude." Candy plucked the book from Clement's hands firmly but carefully, clutching it in both of her hands and thwapping him on the head with it. "You're on a whole new planet, in a whole new galaxy. You have enough money not to work for a *year*. There is literally no reason for you not to write. And you're *good* at it. Don't you want the world to see that?"

Clement wished that life was as simple for him as it had always been for Candy. Her parents loved her, accepted every tiny whim she'd ever expressed from the day she was born. Her sweet father who fainted at the sight of blood was more than willing to let her practice tattooing on him when she decided at age fifteen that she wanted to be a tattoo artist. Luckily, she never got quite that far.

He wondered what that was like, to have your loved ones' blind support that you'd be incredible at anything you put your mind to. Clement's mother never read a word of his writing, and he wasn't sure she would've even liked it if she had.

He raked his fingers through his hair, pushing his fringe from his eyes. "It's not that simple, Candy," he said quietly. "I have to be able to present my best work to agents in *four months*. I haven't written in *five years*."

"You just started again, didn't you? So it hasn't been five years anymore," Candy pointed out.

Clement huffed. "That's not the point."

Candy's shoulders sagged, and he felt bad for bursting her perpetual optimism bubble. "At least think about it, okay? Do something for you. Or if I can guilt you into it, do it for *me*." She fluttered her eyelashes at Clement and he laughed despite himself.

Maybe it wouldn't be the *worst* thing he could do. And Zanna was right. He didn't have to pitch his book. He could just... go. Meet other writers. Be inspired.

Or would it be a waste to go and *not* try to land a publishing deal? "Fine, fine. I'll *think* about it," Clement said, and Candy narrowed her dark lined eyes at him, holding out her pinky.

"Pinky promise?"

Clement smiled. "Pinky promise."

Chapter Five

Qaed

QAED COULDN'T SLEEP.

He was no stranger to insomnia, but that didn't mean he'd ever really learned how to handle it. A lot of the time, he'd go out, but he wasn't sure he felt up to that tonight. His comm read 3:04 am–a lot of the night's parties would be dwindling by this point anyway.

So he found himself on the treadmill in his room, because what else would he do? He'd probably meet up with Jorai in a few hours anyway, so he might as well get a workout in beforehand. He adjusted the running pad to a steep incline and started running.

Vendi typically ended up being the victim of his insomniac tendencies, but she always answered. And in any case, she was his littlest sibling–he had to exercise his oldest sibling privileges in some way. Most nights that he called her at this time, she was already wide awake. But her groggy voice filtered throughout the room once she answered. "Good morning, Qaed," she said, stifling a yawn.

"Shit, did I wake you up? I apologize, I thought you would be awake," Qaed said.

"That is fair." Vendi gave in to the yawn this time. "Is everything alright?"

"Just could not sleep. And I have not talked to you in a while." Qaed was close to both of his siblings in different ways; Votra was the most emotionally available of them, which truthfully didn't say much. Vendi, on the other hand, was nearly a carbon copy of Qaed, which frustrated Qaed more than it should. She and Qaed would take missions together, once upon a time. He couldn't let himself think too much about how much he missed it.

"Sorry. I have been pretty busy." Vendi shifted, and Qaed could barely make out the rustle of a blanket over the comm line. "How are things for you?"

This was how their conversations always went. They talked in circles; Qaed never said what was actually going on in his life, and he was pretty sure Vendi didn't, either. He'd give Qaed the short of things–update him on the lives of other bounty hunters they'd both worked with, talk about the new planets he'd visited.

But that was okay, because that meant Qaed didn't have to divulge anything, either. "They are fine. My new roommate moved in last week, and I like him. It is definitely still strange not having Votra here, though."

"What is he like?"

Qaed turned up the speed on the treadmill. "He is one of Candy's friends from Earth, so I think he is feeling a bit lost. But he is...." What could Qaed say? He was funny, charming, *gorgeous*? Exactly Qaed's type? Vendi wasn't the type to rib him about his new found attraction, but he wasn't sure he was ready to speak it into existence just yet. It would be so easy to ignore it, shove it to the back of his mind like he did with everything else. "He is nice. I just hope that he does not get too overwhelmed."

"I was on Earth a little while ago, and I have to say, he made the right choice. There are not enough credits in the universe to persuade me to live there," Vendi snorted. "Poor thing. I hope that he does not have too hard of a time adjusting."

"Me too," Qaed said. "But what about you? What have you been up to?"

"Oh, much of the same. Working, sleeping. Nothing terribly exciting," Vendi said, which felt remarkably like the exact same answer he'd given Qaed before. "I am going out to Corvora tomorrow for a job, and then I am not sure what comes next."

"What are you doing on Corvora?"

"Something about some lab group." Vendi faltered. "You do not want to hear about this."

He did and he didn't. Talking about work made Qaed feel some semblance of normal, even if it also served as a reminder that his life was nothing but normal anymore. "I am asking as your sibling who is invested in your life. Your job is part of that."

"Qaed." Vendi sighed. "It is late, and I have to travel tomorrow. I should go."

Qaed knew Vendi was only trying to protect his feelings, but her efforts only frustrated him. She was shutting him out of something that he had every right to be a part of. His body was the only thing slowing him down. He thought Vendi, of all people, would understand that.

"Yes, of course. Sorry for waking you," Qaed said.

Vendi paused. "You know that I am just looking out for you, right?"

He *did* know, and he wished he could learn how to be appreciative of it. He wouldn't crumble if Vendi dared mention Qaed's old life.

"I know," he said, keeping the rest of his thoughts at bay. "Be safe tomorrow."

"You as well," Vendi said, as she always did. As if there was anything within the walls of this damn apartment that could hurt him.

He cranked up the speed on the treadmill and broke into a sprint. It was short-lived; his chest ached after only a few minutes, so he turned the treadmill off with an irritated huff, bracing himself with a white-knuckled grip on the handrails. He didn't know why he ever thought exercising when he couldn't sleep was a good idea–all it did was give him *more* energy. And the conversation hadn't helped.

He moved into the living room, wiping the sweat from his brow with his shirt, and flipped the lights on. "Jesus!" came Clement's voice from the couch, and Qaed nearly jumped out of his skin.

How long had *he* been there? He was tucked into a corner of the sofa, sitting cross-legged with the strange old terminal in his lap. Clement rubbed at his eyes before resting his bleary gaze on Qaed. "Can you turn the lights back off? It's too bright in here."

"Turn the lights... off? How can you see?"

"I can't. That's kinda the point," Clement said. Qaed flicked the lights back off, his eyes struggling to adjust to the darkness. He was used to a life bathed in light–Alqen, his home, was one giant reflective surface, three planets closer to the sun than Veterok-III.

"Oh, no. Our first roommate squabble," Qaed teased, his shin crashing into the coffee table. "Shit."

Clement barked out a laugh. "Wow, you're *blind*, huh?"

"Shut up." He made his way to the couch and sat next to Clement, tucking his leg under himself. "What are you doing up so late?"

"Couldn't sleep. After dinner, I felt like writing, so... I started and then I just couldn't stop," Clement said.

"Oh yeah? What are you writing?"

Qaed could see Clement's cheeks turning pink, even against the harsh light from his computer illuminating his face. "It's just some silly little romance thing."

"Votra is going to be your biggest fan," Qaed chuckled. "Can I see what you have written?"

"No!" Clement squeaked, all but slamming his computer closed. Qaed immediately missed being able to see his face. "Sorry. It's just really rough right now. I'm *really* out of practice."

Qaed raised his hands in surrender. "Alright, fair enough." He tapped on his comm to turn on one of the dimmer lights, which Clement didn't seem terribly bothered by.

He set his small terminal next to him on the couch, his mouth stretching into a yawn. "I didn't get to properly thank you for dinner last week, by the way. Thank you."

Qaed smiled, his chest growing tight. He couldn't tell if it was from the exercise or the warmth on Clement's face, but either way, he wished it would stop. "Oh, I am hardly worth thanking. It *was* my intention to treat you, but that did not exactly work out the way I wanted it to."

"It's the thought that counts." Clement propped an elbow up on the back of the couch, mashing his cheek into his fist. He bit his lip. "I haven't gotten out like that in a really long time. Like, a *really* long time."

"Honestly? Neither have I." Qaed shifted around to face Clement, and he suddenly wished he'd showered before coming out here. He probably looked a sweaty mess next to Clement's freshly showered self. His dark brown curls were still slightly damp, and he smelled of spices that Qaed couldn't quite place.

"Really? You strike me as the kind of person who goes out a lot," Clement said.

"Not like that." Sure, he went out to clubs on a regular basis. Most of his interactions with others were so muffled by music that he couldn't make out what anyone was saying. And a lot of the time, it didn't matter. They were just going to end up at the other person's place, tangled up in sheets and sweat-soaked clothes.

And usually, that was what he preferred. He wasn't good at conversation, and he didn't want to learn how to be.

"Well, thanks for the invitation," Clement said, casting a sideways look at his computer. "I was thinking about something, though."

"Yeah?"

"You never did look at my Starcrossed matches." Clement grinned. "Do you want to?"

Gods, did he. He loved the mess of dating apps when he wasn't personally involved in it. "I thought you would never ask."

Clement brought up the Starcrossed interface and Qaed shifted closer to him. "Damn, thirty matches?" Qaed asked. A twinge of something sharp twisted in Qaed's chest, and he ignored it in favor of scrutinizing the profile in front of him.

The guy was muscular, taller than Qaed if what he put on his profile was correct. Now that was just unnecessary. Who needed to be *that* tall? His profile picture was more ab than anything, very clearly taken in the *very* dirty mirror of his bathroom. A toothbrush sat out completely raw on the countertop, the bristles nearly decimated. This man's gums *had* to be shredded.

The second picture he scrolled to featured him, mercifully fully clothed, holding a canaeus with six fluffy legs and giant black eyes poking out of a mass of white fur. Qaed couldn't help but think that appealing to the masses with cuteness was cheap, but the little creature *was* cute.

"He looks like he has a soft side," Clement cooed.

Qaed had a soft side, too. Somewhere. Maybe. He scoffed. "Did you read his profile? It says...." Qaed cleared his throat. "My mom says I'm *really* funny and *really* handsome."

"Maybe he's being ironic."

This was going to be harder than he thought. "It gets worse," Qaed said. *Much* worse. "I don't pay on first dates because I work hard for my money and I'm not a meal ticket. I value my time, my energy, and my money, and I'm looking for someone with the same mindset." Gods, he was *actually* going to vomit. "And then it says '#getonmylevel.'"

Clement's nose wrinkled. "Ew."

"And then, to top it all off, the last line says 'Don't hit me up if you're unemployed or you haven't stepped into a gym in the last twenty-four hours.'" Qaed flicked his profile away without a second thought. Clement opened his mouth like he was going to protest, but stopped. "Trust me, it's for the best," Qaed said. "So I am going to wager that your type is borderline problematic, muscular men with a soft side."

"When you say it like that, it sounds gross," Clement whined, burying his face in his hands. "I think muscles are hot. I want a guy who can pick me up, y'know?"

Qaed could *definitely* pick Clement up. Not that he was in the running, of course. Not that he wanted to be. "Sure. Understandable. But surely you would like an iota of emotional intelligence in the mix?"

"Emotional intelligence would be nice," Clement acquiesced. Well, *that* would put Qaed out of the running for sure.

The next profile was a stark difference to Mr. Just Abs; the human didn't appear muscular, or if he was, it was hidden under layers of sweater and scarf. His warm brown skin, big smile and even bigger eyes made him look kind, approachable.

"He's *really* cute, isn't he?" Clement asked.

He was. "And his name is Adonis?" Qaed squinted in the low lighting. "He likes reading, music, animals, and dad jokes. Sure, he sounds good if you are in the market to date *yourself*."

Clement tipped his head back and laughed. "Oh my God, you're right. We're too similar. Dammit. Sorry, Adonis." He swiped Adonis's profile away, and the tightness in Qaed's chest abated slightly.

They went through a few more profiles like that; Clement's bar for men was in hell, and frankly, Qaed was concerned for him. He was doing his part as a good roommate, just like he promised.

"Well, you have plenty of options for some good hook-ups," Qaed said as he flicked away the latest profile. "If that is what you are after."

Clement squirmed next to him. "I'm... not really looking for hook-ups, actually." He leaned his head back against the couch cushion behind him. "I don't know what I'm looking for exactly. But I feel like I need to put myself out there, you know? Maybe it'll help me write more."

"What do you mean?"

Clement scrolled through the newest profile, lingering for a second on yet another picture of the guy with a canaeus. Maybe Qaed should get a canaeus. "Is it shitty of me to say that I wanna go on dates because I think they'll inspire me?"

Qaed sat back a little, tucking his other leg under himself. "Do you want my honest answer?"

Clement groaned. "So *yes*, it *is* shitty."

Qaed didn't think it was. And even if he did, saying so would make him a hypocrite. While his encounters with other men didn't toe into *romantic* territory, they certainly were sexual. And he didn't seek them out for any other reason than his own selfish needs. The need to be distracted, the need to be *wanted* for a night and *only* for a night.

"You need inspiration for your books, is that it?" Qaed asked. "You want to have romantic experiences so that you can write about them?"

"...Yeah, I guess so." Clement pushed his fringe out of his eyes. "Our dumb little fake proposal gave me so many ideas, I've written more in the past week than I have in five years."

Qaed looked back at Clement's comm screen. Aeken, an emerald-skinned drucaro bartender with shaggy black hair and a soft smile, was going to have to wait his turn. "So let me help you," he said. The words were out of his mouth before he could regret them.

Clement blinked. "What do you mean?"

"I mean, if you are looking for something specific... maybe you and I can do it together. If the fake proposal inspired you that much, surely we can manufacture other scenarios that will help your writing, right?"

Clement shot Qaed a wild-eyed look. "No way. You don't have to do that for me. That's asking *way* too much of your time—"

"What, you do not wanna hang out with me?" Qaed teased.

"I didn't say that!" Clement huffed, giving Qaed's shoulder a shove. "I... it feels like a big ask. And I mean, if I go on dates, maybe I'll find the love of my life and then I'll have endless inspiration forever!"

Qaed *really* didn't like how that made his chest feel. Clement deserved to find the love of his life, and maybe offering this to him was selfish. "I am just saying, I would be happy to do this for you. As long as you are paying."

"You still owe me at least *one* dinner, since you didn't pay for the last one." But Clement smiled, a sweet, closed-lipped smile that melted Qaed's insides. "Really? Are you sure this isn't putting you out?"

"Believe me, I do not offer to do things I do not want to do."

Clement's shoulders sagged, and he closed the Starcrossed app in favor of leaning in to hug Qaed. Now he *really* wished he'd showered. "Thank you," he said quietly, goosebumps prickling the skin of Qaed's neck.

"It is no problem. I am not in a position to say no to free dinners."

"You know this isn't gonna be *just* dinner, right?" Clement asked pointedly.

"It is not? Damn. Is it too late to take back my offer?"

"Yes." Clement stood, stretching his arms over his head and giving Qaed a peek of his stomach. He *had* to stop doing that. "I'm gonna try and get some sleep. You should too."

Something told Qaed he wasn't going to sleep any time soon. "Goodnight," he said as Clement gathered his computer into his arms.

"'Night, Qaed."

Chapter Six

Clement

CLEMENT AWOKE THE NEXT morning to the smell of food. His stomach growled in response, and he rolled out of bed with a grunt. God, how long had it been since he'd stayed up that late? He didn't even stay up into the wee hours of the morning as a teenager, never mind as an almost thirty year old.

He threw on the first t-shirt he found in his closet and shuffled into the kitchen, where a much too awake Qaed was standing at the stove... whistling.

With no shirt on.

"Has anyone ever told you it's *really* dumb to cook without a shirt on?" Clement asked, hopping onto the counter beside Qaed. This was a facet of male behavior that Clement still hadn't exactly gotten behind. Maybe it came from twenty-three years of being told that his chest was inappropriate, but he still felt kind of wrong being topless at the beach.

The only thing wrong with Qaed being topless, however, was how hot he was. Clement knew Qaed worked out, but now his muscles were on full display. A long, shiny scar stretched from the base of Qaed's throat to just below his sternum, and he tried not to let his gaze linger on it for too long.

"I have never been one to steer away from a little danger," Qaed said, stirring around a decent pile of purple pepper-adjacent vegetables and greens in a pan.

For some reason, Clement would have expected not to have to do mundane Earth things like cook since he'd been here. He thought maybe civilization in a different galaxy had moved on to being able to make food at the press of a button. But something about seeing his alien roommate cooking on a stove made him feel just a little more at home.

"Are you hungry?" Qaed's voice interrupted his thoughts.

"No, you don't have to make me anything—"

"That is not what I was asking." Qaed's tone was forceful but not unkind, and it was enough to make his heart stutter. "I always make entirely too much food, so you would be doing me a favor if you had some as well."

"Uh, okay, I'll have some. Thanks."

Qaed pulled a container of a chunky sauce the same purple as the peppers out of the fridge and dumped it into the pan. The smell of herbs filled the kitchen, and Clement suddenly felt much more awake than he had a few minutes ago. "Have you put any thought into our conversation from last night?" he asked.

Clement turned to look at him. "Wait, you were serious about helping me? I kind of thought that was an offer made out of sleep deprivation."

"Not at all. Three in the morning is actually a very *normal* time for me to be awake."

Well, Clement's agreement to it had *definitely* been a product of sleep deprivation. Why did he think this was a good idea? On a good day, Clement could hardly function around Qaed because of how stupid attractive he was.

He hummed under his breath in thought. "I mean, I guess *this* is a good start. A lot of romances have cooking scenes in them."

"Well, you are more than welcome to help. There are some *sulta* breads in the fridge that I need, if you do not mind grabbing them. It should be a bag of circular breads."

"Sure." Clement slid off the counter and peeked into the fridge. This was, by far, the healthiest fridge he'd ever seen–packed to the brim with vegetables, not a hunk of meat to be seen. Bottles of some sort of liquid lined the inside of the door. "You cook a lot, huh?"

"I try to," Qaed said. Clement reached for a plastic bag of what looked like flatbread and closed the fridge behind him. "Do you?"

"I used to." Clement opened the bag of bread and was immediately greeted by sharp citrus and warm herbs. "It used to be just me, my mom, and my sister back at home. Neither of them were big cooks, so I made most of our meals." Qaed turned a switch on the stove and one of the flat, glass-shielded plates on the stovetop burned red.

"Same for me. My parents were often not home, and neither Votra nor Vendi can cook to save their lives." Qaed grinned, pointing to the red eye on the stove. "Just throw one of the breads on there to warm it up."

Clement did as he was told, and the heat on the *sulta* bread only served to intensify the delicious smell. "And you *still* like cooking? Now that I don't live at home anymore, I never wanna touch a stove again."

"It is meditative for me. Votra and Vendi always used to offer to help, but I liked doing it alone. It gave me time to think." Qaed moved his pan off the stove and onto the countertop. "How did your mother and your sister feel about you moving out here?"

Clement's stomach lurched. He still hadn't so much as heard from Cecily since he'd gotten here, but that wasn't unusual. He often went stretches of weeks without hearing from her, especially now that she was on tour.

"My mom isn't around anymore, but if she was, I think she'd freak out." She *definitely* would. It wouldn't have even been a conversation in the first place. "But my sister thinks it's cool. She's a traveler too, so she'll probably end up out here at some point." He reached for the bread and flipped it, earning an impressed sound from Qaed.

"Strong hands," he said, and Clement warmed under the praise.

"*Barista* hands. Years of being covered in boiling hot milk really kill the nerves in your fingers." Clement held his hands up and wiggled his fingers, and Qaed chuckled.

"I am sorry about your mother," he said, stepping away from the stove. He maneuvered around Clement, placing a large hand on the center of his back as he reached for the cabinet above him. Even through the fabric of his t-shirt, his skin burned where Qaed touched him. "I did not intend to bring up a difficult topic."

"It's fine," Clement said, taking the plates from Qaed as he passed them to him. "You made me think about my dead mom, I made you think about your absent parents. I think we're even."

Qaed laughed and moved to the other side of Clement again, and Clement plucked the bread from the stove and dropped it onto a plate. "Alright, good point."

Clement tossed another bread onto the stovetop. "Sorry about your parents, though. I'm sure that was hard."

"Many qintaril children raise themselves. There are often elders around to help, but it is not uncommon. Particularly not where I grew up," Qaed said. He scooped a hearty helping of saucy vegetables onto each plate. "I am proud of my siblings and who they became. I did not do too terrible of a job, it seems."

Clement's stomach twisted, and he suppressed the urge to put a comforting hand on Qaed. He related on a level that hurt to talk about. He wasn't solely responsible for Cecily's upbringing; he was more like an equal part to his mother, the father figure in place of the one that left him and Cecily when they were babies.

"I haven't met Vendi, but I know Votra's great," Clement said, placing the second bread on a plate. "They're lucky to have you."

Qaed cleared his throat and handed Clement the plate with the warmer bread. "I hope that you like it. And do not be afraid to be honest. I promise you will not hurt my feelings."

Clement hopped back up onto the counter. Qaed's message was coming across loud and clear–he was done with this conversation, and Clement could respect that.

Qaed moved closer to Clement, his thigh brushing the part of Clement's leg that dangled from the counter. Clement could have sworn all of the blood in his body rushed to his face. He watched Qaed first, who ripped off a piece of the flat bread and used it to scoop up some of the sauce and vegetables. Clement followed suit, popping an entirely too large bite of food into his mouth.

But it was delicious. Savory, spicy, with a hint of bitterness rounded out by the slightly citrus-y bread... he could eat this forever. "Holy shit," he managed around the mouthful of food. "This is amazing, Qaed."

"I know." Qaed grinned, sticking the end of one of his fingers in his mouth and sucking the sauce off. Jesus, did this man know what he was doing? The blood that had once fled to Clement's face was now moving to a very different, further south region of his body.

Clement ripped off a piece of bread and pelted Qaed with it. It hit him square in the cheek and fell onto his plate. "Ass." But he couldn't stop the smile tugging at the corners of his lips.

"You know, that is not the first time someone has called me that." Qaed made a point to pick up the piece of bread that once belonged to Clement and popped it into his mouth, sans any kind of toppings. How pathetic was it that Clement found that intensely intimate?

"Does that ever make you think you should change?"

"Absolutely not. It is part of my charm," Qaed grinned. He crossed his legs at the ankle, taking another bite of food. "So, how was this for *romantic inspiration*?"

Truthfully, Clement had forgotten entirely that this was the whole point. Maybe he should've been taking notes. But it was so hard to focus on anything else when Qaed was talking, especially so vulnerably.

"Well, usually in rom-coms, the love interests end up getting really derailed while they're cooking. Throwing stuff at each other, making a mess of the kitchen–"

"That sounds like a nightmare," Qaed said through a mouthful.

"That's what I thought, too." Clement tried not to stare at the smear of sauce at the edge of Qaed's mouth. "It's kind of cute sometimes, though. Someone always ends up with a little smudge of something on their face, and the other person tenderly brushes it off."

"Do I have anything on my face? You can tenderly brush it off if you want to," Qaed said, turning his head one way, then the other.

Clement's heart hammered against his ribs. "You do. C'mere." Qaed moved in between Clement's legs and Clement reached up, cradling one side of Qaed's face in his hand as he wiped away the sauce with the pad of his thumb.

Qaed's skin was *ridiculously* soft, he noticed immediately. He was all sharp angles from afar, but actually touching him was different. Their eyes caught, and Clement let his gaze linger for just a second before he looked away. "Like that," he said, more breathlessly than he intended.

Qaed didn't speak for a moment. "Oh," he said quietly. "Yeah, alright. I can see the appeal."

So could Clement. Qaed stepped away and Clement shoved a too-big bite into his mouth to give his brain a second to buffer.

Qaed was flustered, too. He could see it in his face. But that was only natural, right? Clement's thumb had all but brushed across his lips, which was *much* more intimate than anyone needed to be with their roommate of just over a week.

Clement polished off the last of his food and stuck his plate into the countertop sanitizer. He felt a bit like he was shoving his plate into a toaster oven, but he didn't think he'd ever tire of pulling a sparkling clean plate out of it. "Thanks for making breakfast," he said, finally brave enough to look up at Qaed.

Whose eyes were focused square on his mouth. "You have sauce on your face, too," he said, and Clement quickly swiped the back of his hand over his lips.

"I'm, uh, probably gonna go write for a while."

"Sure. Enjoy your... writing."

Clement bolted for his bedroom and pressed his back to the door, clamping his hands over his mouth and letting out a squeal.

This man was actually going to be the death of him.

"Shut up," Vandu laughed, chucking a piece of bread at Dholzi. "Asshole."

Dholzi caught it before it pelted him in the face. "What? If you can't take it, don't dish it out." As if to make a point, he popped the piece of bread into his mouth and sat back with a satisfied grin.

Vandu ripped another sizeable chunk of bread from her small loaf and dipped it into the rather unappetizing slurry of grains and some sort of meat on her tray. Dholzi's large hand circled her wrist before she could even ponder her next move. "Think about your next move, Straal," he warned.

Vandu raised her eyebrows. "What were you gonna do if I threw this at you?"

"Do it and find out." Mischief glinted in his dark eyes, and Vandu's breath caught in her throat. She hesitated for a touch too long; Dholzi stole the piece of bread with his mouth, his lips on her fingertips for the briefest second. "Too late."

– Excerpt from *To Spite a Raven's Heart* by Clement Hall

Chapter Seven

Qaed

QAED DIDN'T THINK HE'D ever seen a rom-com in his life, or that he really knew what it was.

Votra had all but forced him to watch her favorite movie, *Outlaw Koran,* when they were young–a high octane, fast-paced action thriller with a hefty dose of romance. And he'd loved it, if only for the blazing guns and leaping out of space shuttles.

After Clement left him alone rather abruptly in the kitchen, he took the remainder of his breakfast to his bedroom. He had to do his research, after all–how could he be of any help to Clement if he didn't even know what a rom-com was?

He texted Votra for recommendations, and she was all too happy to give them.

> You should watch *Meet Me on Mercury*. It is about two strangers who meet on Mercury and drunkenly elope.

> That sounds stressful.

> It is not! It is very sweet. The two are very different and they learn how to understand each other despite their differences.

> Or you could watch *Anyone But You*. That one is about two best friends who casually sleep together and refuse to fall for each other. And then they do.

> You WOULD like that one.

> It is a good movie, my own personal biases aside.

I am surprised you are interested in such movies.

It is… for research purposes.

You are conducting research? About what?

…Never mind. Thank you for your recommendations.

Qaed settled for the first one; maybe watching a movie about two very different people learning to understand each other would help him.

He and Clement were *very* different, after all. Clement was smart. Funny. Maybe a little rude, but in a way that Qaed liked. He was writing an entire *book*. Qaed couldn't even remember the last time he'd read one.

And Qaed was… Qaed. A washed up ex-bounty hunter with a weak heart and terrible sleeping habits. He sighed, setting his plate down on the table next to his bed.

He watched as one of the movie's leads, a pragmatic businesswoman, arrived on Mercury at the famous Fortuna Hotel. She was all fluffy brown hair and attitude, and Qaed found himself liking her immediately. She was at the Fortuna for work–a team building vacation that she was bound to get a big promotion at the end of. There was a lot at stake for her, and she couldn't afford to get distracted. Especially not by the gorgeous orlix receptionist who didn't even try to hide the fact that she was checking her out.

The receptionist made herself available for the businesswoman, letting her open up about her problems and being vulnerable in return. They had a particularly tender scene at one of the Fortuna's most elegant bars that involved both of the love interests opening their hearts to one another about how difficult it was to love when work stood in the way.

"So much of my life has revolved around work," the businesswoman said over her sparkling cocktail. "I've just been so busy, I… I guess drunk me decided that I'd only make time for love if I was legally required to."

Qaed let out a long, irritated groan. "Okay, Votra, message received loud and clear," he said. He had half a mind to turn the movie off, but dammit, he was invested. He *wanted* them to legitimately fall in love. He knew that, within the conventions of the genre, they *would* fall in love, but he wanted to see it.

And the movie delivered. The middle was rife with adorable, sometimes cringe-worthy scenes; learning about each other through drunken trivia nights in the hotel's main bar, the characters not-so-secretly admiring each other in bathing suits at the pool. Vulnerability in fleeting moments, like the businesswoman emerging from her room in the dead of night in a fluffy robe with bags under her eyes. The receptionist was there to offer a listening ear; she always was.

Qaed only teared up a little at the end, when they remarried at a proper ceremony in front of their friends and family. He understood the appeal now; rom-coms were unrealistic on purpose. He couldn't imagine a scenario in which flaying himself open and revealing his heart to anyone would make them *more* attracted to him.

He shoved himself out of bed and into the kitchen with his now empty plate. Maybe he wasn't the right person to help Clement with this. Sure, he could be a body against the backdrop of a fancy hotel or a glittering pool. He would be more than happy to show up in just a swimsuit and lounge by the water for a while. Hells, it'd be an excuse to see Clement in just swim trunks.

He pushed the thoughts back, his body carrying him down the hallway to Clement's door. Maybe he wasn't the most emotionally available guy out there, but this was his job now. He'd show Clement the most tooth-achingly sweet romantic comedy life he could imagine. And then maybe he'd become a famous writer and move into a giant penthouse in one of Veterok-III's wealthier districts, where he wouldn't have to live with a stranger.

He went to knock on Clement's door but it opened just as he raised his fist. Clement crashed right into him, and Qaed instinctively steadied him with an arm around his waist.

"Sorry, I did not mean to–" Qaed started, at the same time as Clement said, "Jesus, you're *still* shirtless?" Qaed retracted his arm immediately and shoved it behind his back. Clement stared directly at the center of Qaed's chest before correcting himself and meeting his eyes.

"Uh, what's up?" he asked.

Qaed leaned against the frame of the door. "Sorry. I walk around shirtless a lot–would you prefer that I do not?"

"...I don't mind." Pink dusted across Clement's cheeks. "It's your apartment, too."

"Right, of course." Qaed rested a hand at the nape of his neck. "I wondered if you might like a change of scenery. I just watched a film that took place at a hotel and it seemed quite romantic to me."

Clement's lips curved into a teasing smile. "You watched a rom-com?" He folded his arms over his chest. "Did you like it?"

"It was alright." He'd probably end up watching it again–for research purposes, of course.

Clement eyed him but didn't argue. "A change of scenery might not be such a bad idea... what did you have in mind?"

Qaed had toyed with the idea of taking Clement to the Fortuna, but he wasn't entirely sure he was up for the day-long journey. Or how appropriate it was to force your roommate of a week into your shuttle for a day-long journey.

"Well, there are a few places we could go," he said. "There is a really nice hotel not far from here that we could go to. I was also thinking about going to the boardwalk. It is a bit further away but the fair is happening right now–"

"A fair?" Clement squeaked, clasping a hand over his mouth. "Okay, yeah. We're going to the fair. I've always wanted to go to one."

Qaed had never really thought much of the fair. It had been fun to go to in between bounty hunting jobs, with his latest paramour on his arm. He'd never gone out of his way to ride the rides or do much more than walk around. It was beautiful, though, if only for the fact that Veterok-III's beaches were stunning.

"I was thinking that maybe we should go at night. Karelia is out right now, and I know you have not seen it yet. There is nothing like the boardwalk under a Karelia sky."

Clement's smile softened, obstructing Qaed's view of his cute, gapped teeth. "That sounds great." He paused. "Thanks. You really don't have to go to all this effort, you know."

"It gives me something to do with my time," Qaed shrugged. Plus, he wasn't sure there was anything he would rather be doing.

"Well, I appreciate it anyway." Clement went to turn back to his room but stopped. "You sure you wanna go? They might force you to wear a shirt."

Qaed grinned. "I think I can handle that this one time."

The boardwalk hadn't changed much since the last time Qaed had been here. It stretched along a decent swath of the lake's shore, dotted with restaurants and souvenir shops. The boardwalk was made of faded, sun-baked stone that was generally too hot to walk on bare-footed during the day. But at night it was cool, a welcome reprieve from the hot sand.

The moment they set foot on the boardwalk, Clement craned his head back, dark brown eyes as wide as the Karelia, Veterok-III's largest moon. Its milky pink face reflected in his eyes, and they seemed to shimmer with wonder. Qaed wished he could take a picture.

"You were right. It's so pretty out here," Clement breathed.

Qaed allowed himself the privilege of staring at him while he was distracted. "I am assuming our moon looks different from yours," he said, leaning his back against the railing.

"Very. Ours is so far away, it's like a little dot in the sky. Yours is so... close. I feel like I could touch it." Clement blinked a few times, as if to physically sever the ties between his eyes and the moon. "I still can't really believe I'm here."

"I know what you mean." Qaed pushed himself off the rail and started to walk towards the fair, Clement falling into step next to him. "Do you like it here so far?"

"It's hard to tell. I've spent most of my time at the apartment. And I guess that hasn't been so bad." He flashed Qaed a grin. "I know I have a lot to see, but at least I have a built-in tour guide now."

"First you ask me for help with your writing, then you force me to be your Veterok-III tour guide? At what point do I get added to your payroll?"

Clement nudged him with his elbow. "I was talking about Candy, you ass." He tucked his hands into the pockets of his jeans, the reflections of the fair's lights dancing on his pale cheeks as they approached. "Though I guess I wouldn't mind seeing the kind of places you hang out. What *do* you do when you're not at home?"

Qaed swallowed, the fair's glowing lights suddenly feeling a bit like a spotlight on him. "Nothing exciting," he said glibly. "I used to go out to bars a lot, but not so much anymore. I work out in the mornings...." Gods, what *did* he do with his spare time? He'd tried going to his regular club about a week after he stopped drinking, and the temptation combined with the fact that the environment was entirely too much without alcohol-induced numbness made it a horrible time. He couldn't even bring himself to go home with Emei without at least one drink in his bloodstream.

Clement had to think he was the most boring man alive. But if he did, he kept it concealed well. "That's one more thing than I usually do," Clement laughed. "Back at home, I used to only leave the house for work. I was hoping that I'd leave more once I got out here... but the thought of it is kinda terrifying."

"Well, since you have appointed me as your built-in tour guide, if there is anywhere you would like to go but do not want to go alone, I would be more than happy to go with you."

"You wanna show me around *so bad,* don't you?" Clement teased, bumping his shoulder into Qaed's. "Okay, consider this your test trial. I've never been to a fair on a different planet before, so... tour guide me."

"Alright. Prepare to be guided." Qaed offered his elbow to Clement and he took it, looping his arm into Qaed's. "Welcome to the Mordov District Fair. This fair has existed for over fifty years, and that ride over there–" Qaed pointed with a finger towards the first ride he saw, a pendulum ride beaming at them with flashing green and yellow lights. "--is the Veterok Whirl. It has existed for as long as the fair has."

Clement's eyes grew wide. "Really? That ride's *fifty* years old?"

"No. But it was convincing, was it not?"

Clement scoffed. "Your score as a tour guide is in the red, just so you know."

"Oh, come on. I was just warming up. Do you not want a personable tour guide?" Qaed looked at Clement, brow raised, and Clement frowned at him.

"...Fine. Continue."

So he did. Most of the fair's attractions were concentrated at one point; the end of the boardwalk, which was where they were. Some of the rides were the same as the last time Qaed had been here, years ago–Clement seemed especially affronted by the thought of a carousel that floated above the fair, taking its passengers along the length of the boardwalk.

"That can't be safe!" he squeaked, and Qaed tended to agree. He'd gone on it once in his life, and even a little tipsy, he'd been terrified that he was going to fall off.

"You do not come to a Veterok-III fair to be *safe*, my dear Clement," Qaed said. "Look over there." He gestured to a small, blue painted building on the opposite side of the boardwalk. "Do you know what an elxid is?"

"No?"

He guided Clement to the building and they both peered in. The building was a single room, circled by stands for spectators. Dozens of people watched as a drucaro clung to a robotic elxid with all four hands. The robotic elxid was a slightly exaggerated version of the real creature–a six-legged reptile with a broad, red-scaled body, a whip-like tail and a narrow, angry face, they were placid in real life but apparently, they looked frightening enough to be the subject of a fairgrounds challenge. The elxid jerked erratically, dashing from one end of the arena to the other in the attempt at bucking its rider off.

"And *that*... is how I broke my horn. You should consider yourself lucky. I do not usually give that information away for free," Qaed said, pulling away from the doorframe.

Clement pulled away, too. "Shut up. That is *not* how you broke your horn."

"Sure is. My friends dared me to take a shot of neverclear–that was my first mistake–and it made me bold enough to try it. I lasted for five minutes and thirty-nine seconds." Maybe that shouldn't have been one of his proudest achievements, but not a lot of people lasted that long. He would've lasted even longer if he wasn't drunk.

"I don't even wanna know what neverclear is," Clement said, his nose wrinkling.

"If anyone offers it to you, do not take it. It could take the varnish off a space shuttle."

"Got it." Clement's eyes flicked up to Qaed's broken horn, and he suddenly wished he hadn't drawn attention to it. "Did it hurt?"

"Oh, like the hells. Our horns are bundles of nerve endings wrapped in bone." Qaed pushed himself off the wall and Clement joined him, surprising him by hooking his hand into the crook of Qaed's elbow.

"That's not so bad. I think it's funny. Hot, buff guy with battle scars from a life of fighting crime is overdone. Hot, buff guy who broke his horn on a *fair ride,* though...."

"You think I am hot?" Qaed nearly stumbled over his words but caught himself. It wasn't like he didn't hear it often; in qintaril terms, he was quite conventionally attractive and he knew it, save for his short stature and broken horn. Even the broken horn worked in his favor sometimes. But something about hearing it from Clement quickened his heartrate.

Clement's lips parted for a moment. "I was just making a comparison, that's all," he said, staring ahead of him. "Can we go on that?"

He pointed ahead of them to a giant glowing wheel; the centerpiece of the fair, the Skylight Wheel was always Qaed's least favorite. It was easily the biggest of the rides on the boardwalk, the top of the wheel completely obscured by Veterok-III's thick, fluffy pink clouds.

And if Clement wanted to go on it, Qaed would too. Because he was a good tour guide.

Chapter Eight

Clement

JUST AS CLEMENT THOUGHT, the wheel ride wasn't too different from a Ferris wheel.

He'd only been on a Ferris wheel once in his life, crammed next to a boy who tried to kiss Clement at the highest point of the ride. Sixteen year old Clement, with a face caked in more makeup than he'd ever need and a dress that clung to him in a way that made him feel ill, pretended to be so absorbed by the view that he didn't realize what the boy next to him was doing.

And now he was going to be on an even bigger Ferris wheel, in the middle of *space,* with a boy that probably wouldn't try to kiss him at the top of the ride. And that was okay. Mostly.

The pods of the wheel were more enclosed than the ones on Earth; instead of leaving the riders exposed to the open air, the pods closed in around them, artificial air pumping in through vents at their sides. But the pod was mostly glass, allowing them a clear view of everything above and below them.

Clement could have sworn he felt Qaed tense beside him. "You alright over there?" he asked, shifting over to give Qaed more room.

Qaed slung his arm over the back of their seat in what Clement could only assume was an endeavor to give Clement more room. He ended up pressed against Qaed's side, which he couldn't say he hated. "Completely fine," Qaed said, his voice terse. The pod shifted and purred to life beneath them, and Qaed flinched.

Was Qaed... *scared?* Clement eyed him, turning to face him. "You don't look fine."

Their pod began its ascent, and Qaed's eyes grew a fraction wider. "I just have not been on a ride like this in a long time," he said.

Was it wrong of Clement to find this endearing? Qaed's broad chest rose dramatically with the effort of drawing in a breath.

"We didn't have to get on this one, you know. Or you could've waited for me," Clement said, casting his attention out to the fair as it grew smaller beneath them. He hadn't realized just how far the boardwalk stretched when he was on land; the stone path embraced the lake's shore for what looked like miles, ending in a small pier where a solitary couple stood. The lake was still, the moon's warm glow reflecting off the glimmering water.

"I had to come with you," Qaed said, and Clement could feel those giant eyes on him. "I would be a terrible tour guide if I had forced you onto the ride alone."

Clement smiled, reaching over to pat the hand that dangled by his shoulder. "Maybe you're not so bad at this after all." His eyes met Qaed's, the moonlight warming his usually stony dark stare. "You're scared of heights, aren't you?"

"No."

"Then look out at the water. It's beautiful."

Qaed turned his head slowly, as if the sight before him would burn straight through his retinas. His chest stilled as if he was holding his breath.

"Okay, okay, you don't have to look out at the water," Clement said quickly, and Qaed wasted no time in looking away. The eye contact he was making was *intense,* even if it was just an excuse not to look down. "Look up, then."

They both tilted their heads back to look up through the glass ceiling as their pod broke through the cloud cover. It felt a bit like they were soaring through cotton candy, and Clement almost wished he could stick his hand out and touch it.

He felt Qaed relax beside him. The sky above them was more beautiful than any skies Earth had to offer; the inky blackness of Veterok-III's night felt darker, deeper than Earth's, like if he went any higher he might disappear into it. A smattering of stars twinkled around them, less stars than he could see from Earth but they were larger, brighter.

"Wow," he breathed.

He'd forgotten what this felt like, to see something so beautiful he wanted to immortalize it in words. It had been so easy to romanticize Brooklyn when he was younger; he lived in the City of Dreams, the Big Apple. Everything he wrote took place in New York City, because why would he want it to be anywhere else? Falling in love in the Big City was the most romantic thing he could imagine.

But he wanted to capture this exact moment in his mind's theater forever, how it felt to be so small, so insignificant in such a massive, magical galaxy an unfathomable distance away from everything he'd ever known.

Next to someone who made him feel slightly less insignificant. Tears prickled behind his lashes and he blinked them away, refusing to allow them to blur his view of such a sight. A comfortable silence fell over them, one Clement wanted to bathe in. He wanted to soak all of these feelings in like a sponge so that maybe, he could recreate them on page.

He didn't know how much time had passed when Qaed finally spoke. "Maybe I am a little bit afraid of heights," he said, the admission drawing Clement so suddenly from his thoughts that he burst into laughter.

"Oh, trust me. I gathered that," Clement said. The stars shimmered in the deep pools of his eyes, and suddenly it wasn't so hard not to be looking at the sky anymore. "Thank you for coming up here with me anyway."

"Do not get used to it. I can assure you I will never be doing this again. My heart cannot take the stress," Qaed said, his lips curving into a smirk. Clement's eyes flicked of their own accord down to where he'd seen the long scar lining Qaed's sternum the other day and wondered if there was truth to his words.

"Don't worry, I'm not strong enough to carry you off the ride if you have a heart attack, so I won't be risking it." He tilted his head back again, the stars slowly fading from view as the ride started its descent.

"Glad we can agree on that." Qaed withdrew his arm from around Clement–around the *seat*–and latticed his fingers together between his knees. "Not a lot of people know I am afraid of heights, so keep it to yourself, alright? I have an image to uphold."

"Oh, right, of course. Wouldn't want anyone to know that big, tough Qaed can be taken down by a fair ride." Maybe it was delusional of him to feel a little warm at the knowledge that Qaed had entrusted him with something so personal, but that didn't stop the warm tingle spreading through his chest. "You like to be mysterious, huh?"

"Something like that." Clement's attention had been drawn by the lake again, but Qaed was still looking up, giving Clement a clear view of his muscular neck and defined Adam's apple. "So has this been helpful for you? The change of scenery, I mean?"

"It has, yeah," Clement said. All he wanted to do now was go home and write, though he wasn't entirely sure all of the inspiration flowing through him was thanks to the scenery. "I feel like I'm starting to get somewhere. I haven't felt this inspired to write in... years. I guess all I had to do was get out of my house."

"What stopped you before?" Qaed asked.

The comfortable warmth that had settled into all of the cracks and crevices in Clement's body suddenly started to feel a little *too* hot. "So much. My mom was sick, and I spent pretty much all of my time just... taking care of her and working. I didn't have the time."

Qaed made a quiet noise of understanding. A lump formed at the back of Clement's throat, and he tried his best to swallow it down. "I wanted to have a book published by the time I was thirty. That was what got me through my twenties. I thought, *I'm gonna go into my thirties and be a published author and then it'll only go uphill from there.* And then my twenties were kind of just... lost to everything else and suddenly, I turn thirty next month."

Qaed was quiet for even longer this time, and Clement sucked in a breath. "Sorry. You didn't ask all that. I got a little caught up in the moment, I guess," he said quickly.

"No, do not apologize," Qaed said, his voice soft but firm. "But for what it is worth... I understand how it feels to have a plan that suddenly does not pan out the way it should have. Sometimes the world is cruel and unfair and no matter how hard you try...." He swallowed, and Clement watched the bob of his Adam's apple.

Not the time, Clement. "Not so far from unlocking that tragic backstory, huh?" Clement said in a desperate attempt to clear the air. It was one thing to allow himself to wallow in his sadness, but he didn't want to bring Qaed along, too.

"It will take a lot more than one fair ride to get my 'tragic backstory' out of me," Qaed said, the corner of his lips quirking into a smile. "Nice try, though."

The ride came to a halt at the bottom of the wheel, and Clement had never seen someone jump out of a seat as quickly as Qaed did. He laughed, taking Qaed's offered hand to help him up. His hand was much larger than Clement's, and much colder. After such a long time of being pressed against Qaed, he needed that cold.

"Okay, so there's one thing that *always* happens in cute little fair scenes like this," Clement said, tucking his hands into his pockets. "You know those little booths where you have to shoot at targets and if you shoot enough of them, you win a prize?"

"Like that one?" Qaed pointed at a booth a few feet from them, surrounded by plush toys in shapes Clement had never seen before. The biggest of them was something that kind of looked like a bear but also *really* didn't–its plush purple fur stuck out in all directions, its four eyes taking up nearly its entire face. A stout nose sat right in the middle of the eyes. It had four short, stubby arms and two slightly longer legs, each ending in bear-like paws. Two long ears like those of a rabbit hung at either side of its head. It was so ugly it was almost cute.

Clement needed it immediately. "*Exactly* like that one."

"So now I have to win something for you?"

"Yep." Clement raised his eyebrows at Qaed. "Unless you can't handle the challenge."

"I most certainly can. Just you wait." They approached the booth, and Clement swore Qaed's chest was puffed out a little. Rows of tiny little monsters moved slowly across a large screen behind the booth attendant, each of them letting out periodic tiny roars. He almost didn't want to see Qaed shoot them. "I would like to try a round, please," Qaed said to the attendant, tapping his comm to a small, tablet-sized terminal before taking the blaster offered to him.

"Alright, don't mess this up," Clement said. "My whole novel writing career rests in your hands."

"Right. I will try not to feel *too* pressured by that," Qaed said, squaring his shoulders. He raised the scope of the blaster to his eye and closed the other. He was taking this *entirely* too seriously, but he looked ridiculously hot doing it.

The blaster let out comical *pew*s as Qaed shot, the tiny monsters exploding with each sound. Damn, he really *was* good at this. "Okay, showoff," Clement scoffed, and Qaed laughed.

By the time the game ended, every poor little monster had been blown to smithereens. "You want that one, right?" Qaed asked, pointing to the giant plush alien. The attendant pulled it down and passed it to Qaed. "How terribly opposed to me keeping it would you be? Now that I am looking at it... I am becoming attached."

"You can keep it, but you better keep your bedroom door locked because I'm gonna come in and steal it," Clement said, holding his arms out. Qaed placed it in his arms and Clement immediately pulled it close, burying his nose in its plastic-scented fur. "He's so ugly. What *is* he?"

"Genuinely, I could not tell you," Qaed said, giving one of its arms a little tug. "He *is* quite ugly."

"Hey. Only *I* can say that." Clement tucked the plush's head under his chin as they started to walk back down the boardwalk. "Okay, it's official now. You're the perfect book boyfriend. Now all I have to do is write a book about *you* and it'll probably be a best seller."

"I can guarantee the galaxy does not want to read a book about *me,*" Qaed said, taking one of the plush's ears in his hand and poking Clement in the face with it. Clement swatted his hand away, but he was relentless.

"Stop, that tickles," Clement whined, stopping in his tracks and grabbing Qaed's wrist. "Just kidding. You're definitely *not* book boyfriend material."

"I never claimed to be." Qaed grinned, his eyes flicking down to Clement's hand. "So when do I get to know what this book you are writing about me is about?"

"It's *not* about you." Not... entirely, at least. Just inspired. Heavily. "I dunno. I guess I could polish up some of it and let you read it. If I'm gonna take it to this conference at the end of the year, I better get used to having more eyes on it."

"Conference?" Qaed asked, and Clement dropped his wrist upon realizing he had been holding it for entirely too long.

"Yeah. The cashier at the bookstore told me about it." He sighed, pulling off to the side to plop on one of the benches lining the boardwalk. Qaed sat next to him, stretching an arm over the back of the bench. "There's supposed to be a pitch event there. So I'd take my book and present it to some people who might want to publish it."

"Wow. That sounds...."

"Terrifying?" Clement exhaled a laugh through his nose.

"Yes. Very," Qaed said, and Clement narrowed his eyes at him. "You can always practice on me, if you would like. I promise to be a very impartial judge."

Clement couldn't help but wonder why Qaed was being so helpful. What was he getting out of this? "You're slowly winning back *book boyfriend* status," he said, punching Qaed in the arm with the plushie's clawed paw.

"Just make sure you do not forget about me when you are a fabulously wealthy author with legions of his own book boyfriends."

Clement didn't think anything could make him forget about Qaed. "You'll always be the first one. That means you *have* to be my favorite."

"I will hold you to that," Qaed said.

Dholzi fumbled with the lantern with trembling fingers. Vandu reached over, her fingertips brushing his as she flicked it on, the faux flame coming to life. She huddled next to him, wrapping both of her green-skinned arms around herself. "You okay?" she asked, taking the thin blanket from her bedroll and wrapping it around both of them. "Yep. Totally cool," Dholzi said, pulling his knees to his chest and burying his face in them.

Vandu stared at him, fighting the urge to push back the curls that had fallen in front of his ears. "You don't look totally cool," she pointed out.

"Yeah, well." Dholzi huffed. "I don't... love the darkness."

"Isn't Tugiri really dark?"

"Are you judging me right now?"

Vandu grinned. "No. Promise." She turned the lantern up a notch, the artificial light bathing their tent. "I think it's cute that you're so scared of the dark. Especially considering you literally fought off a drergin, like, two hours ago."

Dholzi lifted his head, the harsh light of the lantern casting sharp shadows along his face. She wanted to trace her fingers along every line, every curve of him. "Well, you can see a drergin. You can't see what's going on in the dark."

– Excerpt from *To Spite a Raven's Heart* by Clement Hall

Chapter Nine

Qaed

QAED COULDN'T TELL IF he was glad or not that Clement was inspired–over the next few weeks, he definitely felt Clement's absence. He spent a lot of his days holed up in his room, occasionally coming out to have writing dates with Zanna or for food when he could tell Qaed was cooking. Qaed went out of his way to cook more at home during those weeks. Their meals together would be Clement's self-imposed breaks from writing, and he'd give Qaed the occasional nugget about what he was working on.

But today, when Qaed returned from a day out with Vendi, Clement was on the sofa in just boxers and a too-big black t-shirt, a mug between his hands. Something was playing on the television and Clement was so wrapped up in it, he didn't seem to notice Qaed's presence.

"Gods, I was starting to forget what you look like," Qaed said as he closed the door behind him.

Clement paused what he was watching, a grin playing across his lips. "I finished the book," he said. "Okay, it's *far* from finished, but I finished the first version of it. So I'm taking a little break so I can look at it with fresh eyes later." He raised his mug up at Qaed. "I even went out and bought some alcohol to celebrate!"

Qaed faltered. He hadn't drank in months now, and while the idea of celebrating with Clement was enticing, it wasn't a slope he was ready to slide down again. "That is incredible, Clement," he said, settling into the opposite corner of the couch. "You must be proud of yourself."

"I am." Clement stared into his mug. "I thought I'd forgotten how to do this. I really didn't think it was gonna come back to me, but... I just haven't been able to stop. And now I feel like my eyeballs are gonna fall out of my head."

Qaed laughed, tenderness settling into his chest. "So now, instead of looking at your computer screen, you are looking at a television instead?" he teased.

Clement shoved himself off the couch, mug in hand. "Yep. But at least I don't have to use my brain." He lingered for a moment, his eyes on Qaed. "You wanna watch a movie with me?"

"Sure." He didn't really have plans for the rest of the evening, but even if he did, he would have changed them for Clement. He stood as well. "Let me just go and put on some comfortable clothes."

He went back into his bedroom and shed his jeans and t-shirt in favor of his favorite pair of sweat pants and a tank top. The idea of an evening spent curled up on the couch with Clement, watching what was probably going to be a romance movie made his heart stutter. Gods, was he a teenager again?

When Qaed returned to the living room, Clement was back on the couch and a second mug sat on the coffee table in Qaed's spot. "I made you a drink. I hope you don't mind," Clement said, lifting his own to his lips. "I don't really know much about the liquor you have out here, so I just kinda... tried. But it doesn't taste too bad."

All of the heat in Qaed's body rushed to his face. He hadn't had to have this conversation with anyone yet—most of the people in his life were unfortunately all too familiar with some of Qaed's worst habits. Habits that he'd managed to kick before they became *real* problems, but they'd toed the line a little too closely.

It had been all too easy to drown out his worst days with alcohol. Whenever a feeling cropped up that he didn't want to think about, he wouldn't. He'd drink enough that thinking didn't happen, his mind so fragmented that all of the hard stuff just... slipped through the cracks. He swallowed, making a point not to look at it as he sat down. "I... do not drink, actually," he said, and Clement's face immediately paled. "Sorry to have wasted your alcohol–"

"No, no, I should have asked! I'm so sorry, Qaed," Clement babbled, hopping up from his seat and snatching the mug in front of Qaed. "I'll get rid of it, no worries." He disappeared into the kitchen and Qaed heard the drink being dumped in the sink. A fleeting moment of regret fluttered in his chest.

"It is not a big deal, I promise," Qaed said as Clement returned.

"Still, I should've asked. You haven't had alcohol in the house the entire time I've lived here." Clement reached for his own mug. "Is it okay for me to drink around you?"

The question paused Qaed for longer than he wanted it to. Clement took his silence as a no and dumped his own down the sink as well.

And now, all he wanted to do was go back into his room. But he couldn't let Clement have gotten rid of his drink for nothing, so he tucked himself into the corner of the couch again, and when Clement sat down again, he sat closer to Qaed than he had before. The herbal, sweet smell of *ehrai* wafted off him, and Qaed couldn't tell what was more distracting, the scent or Clement being this close to him. He'd done more than his fair share of *ehrai* shots in his day.

"I am not a recovering alcoholic or anything," Qaed said. He didn't know why he was talking. "Not... technically. It was more of a dependency than anything." *Spoken like a true alcoholic,* he told himself.

"You don't have to talk about it," Clement said quietly, his eyes infuriatingly soft on Qaed. "You don't owe me an explanation."

Strangely, Qaed *wanted* to talk about it. But he couldn't handle the way Clement was looking at him with those watery, pitying eyes and a face full of guilt. "You can continue watching your movie if you'd like," he said, and Clement seemed to get the message. He unpaused the movie and sat back, his thigh barely brushing Qaed's.

It looked like Clement was maybe halfway through the movie; the love interests shared their first kiss in the rain, something Qaed couldn't help but think would be *wildly* unromantic with Veterok-III's ice rain. Clement let out a quiet 'aww,' and Qaed smiled despite himself.

He didn't know what possessed him to start talking again, but once he started, he found it hard to stop. "I used to drink when I felt even remotely sad. And for the last few years... I have been sad more often than not." Clement went to pause the movie, but Qaed placed a hand on top of the one holding the remote. "My life has changed a lot from what I expected it to be. And I thought I was handling it well, shoving all of the feelings down and numbing them with alcohol. But, believe it or not, that is not the most healthy coping mechanism."

Clement didn't look at Qaed, for which he was grateful. But Qaed allowed himself to watch the reflection of the movie dance off Clement's soft features. "If it makes you feel any better, my coping mechanism for my life turning upside down was moving to a totally different galaxy." Qaed laughed quietly, swallowing back the lump forming in the back of his throat. "Sorry. Not about me."

"It is alright. It makes me feel better to know that I am not the only disaster in this room," Qaed said, earning him a jab in the ribs from Clement's elbow. "I am fine, though. This is just... a relatively new development for me, so temptation is still... difficult for me."

"Got it. I won't keep alcohol around anymore." Clement leaned into Qaed a little, his back pressing against Qaed's chest. He wasn't quite laying against Qaed, but Qaed had the urge to pull him in closer anyway. "Thanks for telling me. You can be honest with me about stuff, y'know."

"What, and give you more fodder for your tortured book boyfriend's tragic backstory?" Qaed teased.

Clement whipped around, a frown tugging at his lips. "I wouldn't do that, Qaed," he said, his voice more serious than Qaed expected. "It's one thing to do these dumb, fake dates with you, but I would never use your real trauma in a book."

Guilt settled in the pit of Qaed's stomach like a stone. Clement twisted at the waist, the movie behind him completely forgotten. "I promise, your secrets are safe with me. I would never in my life betray your trust like that."

Qaed clenched his jaw against the tears threatening behind his eyelids. Damn Clement. Damn him for being so charming, so kind, so funny, so.... So unlike anyone Qaed had ever met.

"I believe you," Qaed said quietly, drawing in a shaky breath that betrayed the weak composure he was fighting to regain. "Sorry. I was not trying to make an assumption about you."

"Yeah, you were just deflecting with humor. Which you do a lot." Clement smiled, and it was only then that Qaed noticed his own eyes glistening, too. "I *might* have already stolen that trait for my love interest. It's one of the most charming, yet equally annoying things about you. Book boyfriends need to be *balanced*."

"Glad that I could be of service," Qaed said. He could have sworn Clement leaned even closer into him; their chests were practically touching now, Clement shifted around so that his thighs were in full contact with Qaed's. Qaed rested a testing hand on the nape of Clement's neck, and Clement didn't pull away. In fact, it seemed to only encourage Clement to lean into him even more.

"Qaed...," Clement whispered, one of his soft hands coming to rest on Qaed's cheek. "Are you trying to make a move on me right now?"

"What could be more romantic than this?" Qaed asked. "On the couch, a movie playing in the background... both of us on the verge of tears...."

Clement laughed, brushing his thumb across Qaed's cheekbone. "You're right. Like something right out of a movie. Vulnerability is romantic." His eyes flicked down to Qaed's lips, and Qaed took the liberty of leaning in closer, nearly closing the distance between them.

"So, for research purposes... we should kiss right now, right?" Qaed asked.

"I think so. I think it's kind of necessary."

Qaed couldn't tell who was officially the one to initiate the kiss. All he knew was that once it started, he didn't want it to end.

Chapter Ten

Clement

CLEMENT'S FAVORITE PART OF any rom com was the first kiss. It said so much about the couple, set the stage for the rest of their relationship–the first kisses between friends turned lovers were always softer, more gentle. First kisses between friends with benefits, though... their *first* kisses may not be that important, but that first kiss after realizing their feelings for each other was always so damn satisfying.

The best ones, though, were the kisses that felt equally as out of left field as they did so incredibly right. Like the walls of the 'will they, won't they' had finally crumbled.

Just like this one.

Clement didn't move closer to Qaed. He didn't trust himself to. Qaed, however, moved with the confidence of someone who had kissed more than just the one boyfriend he'd had in high school. He snaked a hand into Clement's curls and, for a second, Clement wanted him to tug on them.

His hands shifted from Qaed's face to land on his chest, his firm, muscular chest that was rising and falling much faster than it normally did. He should stop. Maybe things were getting weird at this point. Going out on silly little dates for inspiration was one thing, but kissing him? Wanting to do *more* than kiss him?

As if reading his mind, Qaed pulled away, but just enough to say that they weren't technically kissing anymore.

Say something, Clement. Use your words. He floundered, the darkness in Qaed's eyes not entirely helping that situation. His hands skimmed down Clement's sides, leaving a trail of flames in their wake. All Clement wanted to do was rip his shirt off and feel Qaed's hands on him for real.

But that was putting him into *especially* dangerous territory. Wanting more than this was just setting himself up for failure. Or heartbreak. Sleeping with his roommate was a recipe for disaster. Falling for him *had* to be even worse.

It seemed, though, that his body and his brain weren't on the same page, or even the same chapter. He kissed Qaed again and Qaed fell back into the cushions, spreading his legs to allow Clement to slide between them.

And he took the opportunity immediately. He flattened himself against Qaed, his chest against Qaed's torso. Something firm pressed into Clement's stomach, and he tried not to let himself think about it too much. Especially when he was just as hard against his own boxers.

Fuck, he shouldn't want this. But every hot, needy fiber of his body did. Qaed's tongue slid across Clement's lower lip and he parted them willingly. Their tongues tangled together, Qaed's cold against his own.

Qaed's hands settled on the small of Clement's back, tugging the hem of his shirt up slightly to allow them to rest on his bare skin. Every hair on the back of his neck stood on end at the cold intrusion. Clement shifted upwards, drawing himself closer to Qaed to deepen the kiss, if that were even possible.

And as he did so, the bulge under him that was *definitely* Qaed's boner brushed across his stomach. Clement couldn't withhold his moan if he tried. The sound tightened Qaed's grip in his hair, which only drew another pitiful sound from him.

Shit. Clement ripped himself away from Qaed, hands on his chest as if to push him away. But *God,* did he really not want to. "Sorry. I–"

"I did not mean to–" Qaed spoke at the same time, his breaths shallow.

Looking at Qaed was almost painful; he could tell that every nerve in his flushed body was standing at attention, and Clement longed to trail his fingers down the length of that broad chest, the ridges of his muscular torso, right down to the tent in his pants–

There were very clearly *two* solid outlines of needy dick in his sweatpants, which did very little to quell the desire throbbing between Clement's legs. It would be so easy to put his hand on them, to palm him through his pants like he so clearly wanted.

Clement sat back, raking his fingers through his now disheveled hair. The silence that fell over them was entirely too loud, and Clement silently begged Qaed to say something. Anything. Or to shove Clement against the couch and have his way with him. He'd be okay with that, too.

Or would he?

God, all Clement had managed to do tonight was bring up Qaed's trauma, and now he was gonna leave him alone on the couch with *two boners.* "I-I think I'm gonna go to bed," he said, scrambling to his feet. His erection brushed against the seam in his boxers, and it took everything in him not to moan again.

"It is only six," Qaed said, blinking a few times. He was holding a pillow over his crotch now, making it much easier for Clement to convince himself to leave.

"Yeah. Uh, that alcohol really got me," he said, his mouth stretching into a fake yawn. "Thanks for the, uh...." The kiss that *still* had his lips tingling? The raging hard-on that he was definitely gonna have to go into his room and take care off immediately?

"Of course, it was my pleasure," Qaed said awkwardly, averting Clement's gaze. "Make sure you drink plenty of water. An *ehrai* hangover is no joke."

"Right, yeah. Thanks." Clement scrambled back to his room as quickly as he could, the awkward exchange doing nothing to damper his arousal. He closed the door behind him and groaned. Even though he was far from tired, there was no way he was going to be able to face Qaed again tonight. Or maybe ever.

Especially after what he was about to do. He went into the bathroom and turned the faucet on as cold as it would go, sticking his hands under the flow of icy cold water. Water got *much* colder out here than it ever did on Earth.

He kept his hands there for as long as he could manage before turning it off and dashing into bed. He didn't allow himself even a second of warm-up, lest his hands return to their regular temperature too quickly. His cold fingers against his cock were jarring at first, and the muscles of his lower back clenched against it. But as soon as he closed his eyes and replaced his two cold fingers with the image of Qaed's, the cold became easier to appreciate.

Clement tugged his length between his thumb and two fingers, the digits already coated with his own arousal. Much to his dismay, the hand between his legs warmed up quickly, but the one he splayed across his chest was still as cold as Qaed's.

He wondered if Qaed was doing the same thing. Was he in his room now, cocks in hand, touching himself at the thought of Clement? He probably had more self control than that... but Clement found himself hoping he didn't.

He pushed his hips up against his hand, biting his lip to stifle the moans threatening to spill out. He wasn't sure he'd ever been this aroused in his life.

He slipped a finger into his slick entrance, his own slender finger no replacement for one of Qaed's thick ones. Even the introduction of a second one left Clement feeling empty. At this point, he was starting to wonder if the only thing that would satisfy him was being full of both of Qaed's cocks.

The thought drew a moan from him that he couldn't stop. He slipped a third finger in, the heel of his palm flat against his cock. "Shit, Qaed," he gasped out before he could register what he was saying.

Well, this was definitely a new low for him. But there was no turning back now. He fully leaned into it, lifting his hips off the bed as he imagined his own fingers as one of Qaed's cocks, filling him to the brim.

The comm on his wrist pinged and he ignored it, desperately clinging to his mind's version of Qaed. When it went off again, Clement imagined it was Qaed, waiting outside his door, begging Clement to let him in and finish the job.

Which was easily one of the more pathetic thoughts he'd ever had. He whimpered, dragging his free hand down to his cock and stroking it while he pumped his fingers in and out of himself. He could let himself be pathetic for one night–Qaed didn't have to know. No one did.

And then he'd have it out of his system and he and Qaed would go back to normal. To just regular old roommates who *didn't* think about fucking each other and *definitely* hadn't ever kissed.

His thighs trembled as his orgasm crested inside him, cum spilling over his fingers. He wondered if Qaed was a talker in bed. Would he praise Clement, tell him how pretty he looked when he came? Would the sight of Clement coming send him over the edge, too?

The dream scenarios nearly had Clement ready for another round, but he wasn't sure his ego could take the hit. He withdrew his fingers from himself with a shudder and ran himself the coldest shower he could handle. It was good for his hair, after all.

It did little to calm him down, because apparently he'd developed some kind of Pavlovian response to being cold. "What the fuck, Clement?" he muttered to himself, padding into his bedroom to pull on a fresh pair of boxers and a sleep shirt. He was *definitely* awake now.

His comm buzzed again, and he finally glanced down at it.

> I truly am sorry for making you uncomfortable. I lost myself back there and I should not have.

He sent that thirty minutes ago. *Fuck.* He followed it up with two other messages, which must have been the other two times his comm went off.

> I hope you are alright.

And then the last message was blank, with the words 'message unsent' in its place. "Shit, shit, shit," he whispered. He didn't even *know* comms could un-send messages.

He couldn't leave things like this, not when they lived together. He tugged on a pair of pajama pants–for decency, of course–and left his room to knock on Qaed's door.

The door opened rather quickly, and an equally showered Qaed poked his head out the door. "Hi," Clement said quietly with a little raise of his hand.

"Hi." Qaed opened his mouth as if to speak, and then closed it. "I... should probably not invite you into my room, right?"

"Probably a bad idea after... all that." The thought of being in Qaed's room was so intimate it made Clement's stomach flip. He swallowed as Qaed stepped out the door, also much more dressed than he was before. He'd swapped those slutty gray sweatpants for a pair of thicker black sweats that mercifully hid everything Qaed had going on.

"Right, yeah." Qaed brought a hand up to rest on the back of his neck. "I was worried that I had really upset you."

Sorry, I was too busy jerking off while thinking about you to answer your messages. "I took a shower and didn't see your messages. I didn't mean to make you feel bad," he said instead. "You didn't upset me. Like, at all."

"Oh." Qaed exhaled like he'd been holding his breath. "Good."

Clement carded his fingers through his still-wet hair. Well, this was as good a time as any to just... come out with it. It wasn't as if he could possibly be more embarrassed if he tried. "I'm a virgin and I wasn't sure I was ready. I mean, I *felt* like I was ready but I also felt a little freaked out. N-Not by you or anything, it wasn't you. I got really in my head."

"Sorry, but... what is a virgin?"

Actually, just kill me now. Not only was he admitting *out loud* to quite possibly the hottest man he'd ever met that he was a virgin, he had to spell it out, too? "A virgin is... someone who's never had sex before."

"Ah. That was my assumption, but I just wanted to make sure. Strange that you humans have a word for it, though." Clement's head snapped up to look at Qaed, who was now wearing that annoying smirk that Clement kind of wanted to kiss off his face.

"You are absolutely infuriating," Clement said, but laughed, the tension in his shoulders slowly fizzling out. "I just... didn't want my first time to be on a whim, I guess."

"That makes sense." Qaed leaned his back against the door and pressed one of his fingers to his lips. "I truly am sorry that I pushed things to a point that made you uncomfortable. I got carried away. I knew that you were only looking for a kiss, but I—" He stopped. "I hope that I have not lost your trust."

Clement *wasn't* uncomfortable. If anything, grappling with how badly he wanted this had been the hard part. This was never meant to be more than *research*, which felt shitty now that he was thinking about it that way. "No, you haven't. If it's okay with you, I *would* still like your help with everything. You're kind of a big source of inspiration for me now." Saying that felt just about as vulnerable as if he were to tell Qaed he'd masturbated to the thought of him.

"How could I possibly let you down, then?" Qaed smiled, brushing back a wet lock of hair that clung to Clement's forehead. "I would be glad to."

"Cool. Great. Good talk," Clement said, taking a step back from Qaed. Qaed dropped the hand that had just touched him, tucking it into his pocket. Clement missed it immediately.

Vandu had never kissed anyone before. If she was being completely honest, she wasn't sure she'd ever wanted to kiss anyone before. But as she watched Dholzi with his beer-soaked grin, his heavy-lidded eyes, the arms he was casually throwing around all of their fellow soldiers... she wished those arms were around her.

She stole him away while she could still muster the courage to do so. "Aww. You jealous you're not getting my attention?" Dholzi grinned, leaning in dangerously close to her. She could smell the beer on his breath. "Well, you got me now. All of me." He took another swig from his bottle.

Her heart stuttered. Gods, how she wished that were actually true. How she wished she could give him all of her. She snatched the bottle from him and downed the last half of it, which he started to protest but she didn't give him the chance to. "Kiss me, Dhol."

Dholzi laughed, a small, sharp, surprised sound. "Wh–Huh? Me?"

"No, the other Dhol." Vandu bit her lip. "Unless I've been reading this wrong. In that case–"

Dholzi silenced her with his mouth, two of his hands tangling in her hair and the other two clutching her hips, pulling her closer. She melted into him, wishing this moment could last forever and knowing it never could.

– Excerpt from *To Spite a Raven's Heart* by Clement Hall

Chapter Eleven

Qaed

QAED FOUND HIMSELF AT the gym earlier than usual the next morning. After a fitful night of sleep, he couldn't be bothered to keep trying. Running was the only way to work out the frustration he hadn't managed to work out in the shower earlier.

And truthfully, it wasn't really working. He couldn't get Clement out of his head, the way he'd jumped up from the couch and out of Qaed's arms, his cheeks flushed, eyes wide like he'd been caught doing something he wasn't supposed to.

But being that close to Clement, his soft warmth blanketing Qaed's body, his soft lips against Qaed's and the prickle of his facial hair against Qaed's chin was addictive. He'd wanted to trail his hands across every inch of skin he could reach.

He was being greedy. Clement had asked him for help in a purely research capacity–he hadn't asked for Qaed to have sex with him. And he *especially* hadn't asked for Qaed to be his first, which apparently was important to him. Maybe Qaed wanted to be that important to Clement, too.

"Someone's thinking awful hard," Jorai said, her voice cutting into his thoughts. He nearly stumbled off the treadmill, grabbing the handrails to steady himself. "Don't hurt yourself."

"Gods, since when did you move so quietly?" Qaed stopped the treadmill and stepped off, wiping his forehead with the towel draped around his neck.

"Uh, since never." Jorai stretched one set of muscular arms over her head, the other two resting on her hips as she moved them from side to side. "You okay?"

Gods, he wasn't. He couldn't stop thinking about Clement. Though he didn't feel necessarily *bad* about the way they'd left things last night, he wasn't sure he felt good about it, either. "You should do some cardio this morning," he said, jerking his head towards the treadmill. "Take a break from lifting."

"Fine, but only because I know something you don't." Jorai grinned wolfishly, hopping onto the treadmill. Qaed started up the one next to her.

"Yeah? What is that?"

Jorai looked like she might explode if she didn't tell him right away. "We're going to the Capitol in a few months for a wrestling tournament. With the *Reyes family.*"

Qaed should know who that was. He'd been to more than a few matches of Jorai's, but he couldn't remember a Reyes. "Who is that?"

"Dude, they're wrestling *royalty.* They *founded* the Cosmic Collision Corps."

Qaed turned up the speed on the treadmill, putting him at a decently fast sprint. "And you are going to be wrestling them?"

"Yep. I wrestle Marisol Reyes as the final match on the card. They're, like, the Reyes family crown prince." Jorai turned up her speed as well and Qaed stared pointedly at her in a silent warning. "Which brings me to my question."

He should've known there'd be some ulterior motive. "Turn that down. You need to warm up more."

Jorai huffed, the machine emitting a singular beep as she did so. "I *really* want you to come with me. I've tried other trainers before and they're just not *you.*"

Qaed couldn't entirely tell if Jorai was just trying to butter him up or if she meant it, but he felt himself warming to her words nonetheless. "I am surprised you do not want a trainer who will let you do whatever you want."

"Yeah, well, I feel like I've gotten better since you started training me. I *guess* you were right when you said I should pace myself." Jorai made a point of staring directly at the screen of the treadmill, and Qaed couldn't help but grin. "This match could be really big for my career. I know the results are pre-determined, but... I'd feel better if you were there."

Qaed's stomach swooped. He'd been dodging her requests for months now, but he didn't know she *actually* wanted him there. "Aww. Jorai, you actually like me?"

"If you don't shut up, I'm gonna take it back." Her already red face darkened a few shades, and he suppressed the urge to shut off the treadmill and scoop her into a hug.

Maybe it wouldn't hurt to consider it. He owed it to Jorai, after all. She'd rescued him from the bar after the last time he got drunker than he had any right to be, and she hadn't breathed a word about it since.

Guilt settled in the pit of his stomach. The people in his life had been entirely too gracious with him in these past months; he'd spent so much time *wallowing,* something he'd gotten so good at doing once his one outlet was gone. Jorai hadn't passed so much as a word of judgment on him when she arrived at the gym first thing in the morning to a Qaed who had very clearly already been there for hours.

"Dammit," he muttered under his breath, shutting off the treadmill as tears fogged his vision. Any other day, he would have blinked them back and kept going. But it seemed that, nowadays, his emotions were a little less predictable than they had been in the past. The treadmill whirred to a stop and he lifted the hem of his shirt to wipe his eyes with it. "Yes, Jorai. I will go with you."

"Wait, really?" Jorai asked, and her own machine beeped as she turned it off. "Are you fucking with me right now?"

"Just say 'thank you' before I change my mind." Qaed wasn't going to change his mind, but he'd felt too many things too strongly over the last forty-eight hours. If Jorai was even a little bit nice to him, he'd lose the battle with the tears struggling to break past his eyelids.

Much to his surprise–and chagrin–Jorai wrapped all four arms around him and squeezed him, pinning his arms to his sides. "Thank you," she murmured, and the lump in Qaed's throat grew even harder to ignore.

He sniffed, giving his eyes one quick wipe once Jorai put him down. "I am proud of you, Jorai. I know you have been working hard." He still found it hard to look her in the eye when he spoke. This wasn't the kind of relationship he and Jorai had. But then again, Qaed didn't really have this kind of relationship with anyone.

Up until recently, anyway. "Ew, don't go getting all mushy on me," Jorai groaned, giving his shoulder a weak shove. Her own voice was thick, too, and he couldn't help but think this was why they got along so well.

"You started it with your 'I want you to be there' thing," Qaed said, finally lifting his head to meet Jorai's gaze. All four of her eyes glittered with unshed tears, her stubborn lower lip quivering.

Qaed got it now, why Clement valued vulnerability so much. He felt like he was truly seeing Jorai for the first time, and he tried to ignore how terrifying it was to imagine Jorai feeling the same way about him. "I didn't say I *wanted* you there. I just said I'd feel better if you were there," Jorai said, moving away from Qaed to sit against the wall opposite the machines.

Qaed sat next to her, knees pulled to his chest. "Then I will be there." He turned his head to look at her, nudging her foot with his. "I know that I am not always so upfront about my feelings, but... I am very appreciative of the time we spend together. And of you."

Jorai still didn't quite meet his gaze, her dark eyes fixed on a point across the room. "Yeah. Me too." She bumped his foot back. "Are you dying or something and you just don't wanna tell me? Because this whole... whatever this is isn't gonna soften the blow."

Qaed barked out a laugh. "No, I am not dying. Am I not allowed to tell my friend that I value our friendship?"

Jorai folded a set of arms and rested them atop her knees, then rested her chin on them. "No. You're laying it on a little thick." She shot him one of her brilliant, toothy grins. "You think Clement's gonna be okay all on his own while you're gone?"

Shit. Clement. He had no doubt in his mind that Clement would be fine–if anything happened, he had Candy. But the more troubling part of all this was how badly Qaed *didn't* want to be away from Clement. He must have made a face, because Jorai raised her brows at him. "Ooh. That wasn't a good reaction."

"It was a very *normal* reaction," Qaed said. "It is normal for me to worry about Clement."

"Yeah, that defensiveness was totally normal, too." Jorai snorted. "Trust me, I'm not gonna be the one to lecture you about your love life. Mine is pretty pathetic, too."

"Excuse me." Qaed's love life *was* pathetic, mainly because it didn't really exist. But then again, he hadn't exactly been looking for one. He wasn't the best candidate for any type of relationship. He could hardly maintain the *friendships* he had. He'd be a terrible excuse for a romantic partner.

And up until now, that didn't really bother him. Now... he wondered if he had the capacity to be good for someone. He *hoped* he did.

"Clement will be fine without me." *It is just me I am worried about,* he almost said. He stood with a groan, his muscles protesting now that they were finally at rest for the first time in hours, and reached a hand out to Jorai. "Do you want to keep going?"

"Actually, I think I'm gonna go give Xelith the good news." Jorai grinned, taking Qaed's hand and standing up. "See you tomorrow, though?"

"Of course."

The aroma of coffee greeted Qaed as he stepped into the apartment. "Qaed? Is that you?" came Clement's voice from the kitchen. "Want some coffee?"

He didn't, but he didn't have it in him to turn it down. He kicked his shoes off and went into the kitchen, where Clement was already pulling down a second mug. "Coffee would be nice, thank you," he said, leaning against the counter adjacent from Clement.

"Did you work out with Jorai this morning?" Clement asked, reaching into the cabinet a second time for the sugar that Qaed was definitely going to put in his coffee. The first time he had, Clement hadn't exactly been silent about his distaste for it. He'd stopped voicing it a while ago, but every now and then, his cute nose would wrinkle as he watched Qaed generously sugar his coffee.

"I did." Qaed folded his arms over his chest. "She has a big match coming up in a few months and she asked me to come with her as her trainer."

Clement's hand stopped in mid-air as he reached for the kettle. "That's amazing, Qaed," he said, his hand finishing its journey to the kettle. "Are you excited?"

"I am." He eyed Clement, the look on his face unreadable. "Will you be alright on your own?"

"I think I can manage without you for a little while." Clement poured hot water over the coffee grounds in slow, meditative circles. "Do you know exactly when you're going?"

"Not yet, why?"

Clement's gaze didn't shift from the coffee. "Oh, no reason. I was just...." He huffed out a sigh. "I was gonna ask you if you wanted to come to my writers' conference with me. You don't have to, but... y'know, I need a ride, and you're the easiest person to ask. Plus, Candy's flying kinda scares me."

Qaed's heart leaped into the back of his throat. "I will find out from Jorai and let you know," he said. "But... if the events do not clash, then I would love to go with you."

"Yeah, of course. I wouldn't expect you to pick my thing over yours or anything. A-And don't worry about paying for anything if you can go. It's all on me. You know, to thank you. For everything."

Qaed didn't like this, how awkward things suddenly were. And it was all his own making. "You do not have to do that," he said, watching Clement's hands as he poured coffee into their mugs. He put four spoonfuls of sugar into Qaed's, exactly how he liked it, and passed it to him. Their fingers brushed, Qaed awkwardly wrapping his larger fingers around Clement's as he took the mug from him. The touch sent a jolt of electricity up Qaed's arm.

"I want to." Clement stared at their joined hands for a moment before tugging his own away. "It's the least I could do."

All Qaed could think was that Clement was constantly doing things for him. Making him coffee, remembering how he liked it. Standing with him in the kitchen while he cooked, being a willing taste-tester. Picking up Qaed's favorite meal whenever he got food for himself from Cafe Strelka, even if Qaed said he didn't need it.

Qaed's skin suddenly felt too tight, too small for his body. "If anything, it is I who should be returning the favors. I do not know how I ever made it here without you." He cleared his throat. Maybe his conversation with Jorai this morning had emboldened him *too* much. "And without your coffee. Is this stuff addictive?"

"Actually, yeah, it is. The caffeine in it–the thing that gives you energy–*is* addictive. Pretty much everyone in America is addicted to it." Clement dragged his fingers through his hair. "For the record, I don't know how I would've made it here without you, either."

"You have Candy. You would have been fine," Qaed said.

"Yeah, but... you're different." Clement drew in a slow breath, shifting his gaze up to Qaed. "I wrote a whole book about you."

If Qaed's heart beat any faster, he was certain it would burst through his ribs. "Wow, subtlety is not your strong suit, is it?" he teased, though his voice betrayed him. He still couldn't bring himself to believe that Clement was this inspired by Qaed doing nothing but existing.

"Not really. Us artistic types tend to be dramatic." Clement's eyes flicked down to Qaed's lips, and Qaed instinctively parted them, his lungs suddenly too small to take in as much oxygen as he needed. "I could write pages about that... thing you just did."

"You mean breathing?" Though, he didn't really feel like he was doing much of that. Clement was entirely too close to him while simultaneously being *too far* from him. "Wow, you really should get out more."

"Shut up," Clement laughed breathlessly, taking a small step closer to Qaed. "I don't need to go out. My built-in book boyfriend is right here."

Knowing that Clement wasn't using the word *boyfriend* legitimately didn't stop the swirl of excitement in the pit of Qaed's stomach. "Lucky you."

"Lucky me." Clement turned, fully facing Qaed now. If he took even a step closer, he'd be directly between Qaed's legs. Somewhere Qaed had no right wanting him to be. "Qaed, about last night."

Dammit. This wasn't over. "Clem–"

"Hold on." There was a finality in Clement's voice, a commanding that Qaed's cocks answered to. "I wanna ask you something that you can say no to."

Qaed blinked. He wasn't sure he'd ever be able to say no to Clement. "Okay."

"Things were... going somewhere last night. I wasn't imagining that, right?"

"...They were, yes," Qaed said, his voice small.

"What if... what if we had kept going?" Clement squirmed as if his body couldn't handle the words coming out of it. "It's really hard to write about that kind of thing without having experienced it, and–"

"Clement, we stopped because you did not want your first time to be on a whim." As badly as Qaed wanted to pull Clement into his arms and carry him right into his bedroom, he couldn't bring himself to. "Do you really want your first time to be for *research?*"

Clement drew in a deep breath. "I thought I didn't. But after last night... I dunno." He stepped into the space between Qaed's legs, his hands resting on the counter at either side of Qaed's hips. "Am I crazy to think it felt... right?"

Qaed's brain ceased to function the moment Clement's thumbs brushed his hips. "Sounds like someone's thinking with the wrong head," he teased, his voice thin.

But he wasn't a strong enough man to say no. Not to Clement. "You are absolutely certain you want this?" he asked. "With me?"

Clement paused, and Qaed's stomach rolled. He couldn't live with Clement regretting this. "Yes," Clement finally said.

Everything in Qaed told him to back out. Clement deserved the first time he'd always dreamed of, whatever that was. But when Clement's hands found his chest, his resolve shattered. He took Clement's face in his hands, a silent question that Clement answered by pressing his lips to Qaed's.

Chapter Twelve

Clement

CLEMENT HAD ENVISIONED HIS first time so many different ways. When he was a teenager, he wanted the romance of it. He was so convinced he'd be different, he'd be the one of his friends who would be taken on a rose petal-covered bed, haloed by candles. He wouldn't be the victim to sloppy, awkward first-time sex with clumsy, wandering hands and kisses with too much tongue.

And now, as an adult, he didn't need the rose petals. He didn't really know *what* he needed. But it was easy to convince himself that Qaed was part of it, whatever it was.

Qaed's hands on him were tentative, once again slipping up the back of his shirt to rest against his skin. He shivered, pressing his chest against Qaed's. Qaed's lips parted in a gasp as Clement's crotch met his, and Clement took the opportunity to slide his tongue past them.

As if flipping on a switch, Qaed came to life under his hands. The kiss turned hungry in an instant, his cold tongue tangling with Clement's. Clement whimpered, arousal curling in the pit of his stomach. The sound seemed to spur Qaed on, his hands moving down to grasp handfuls of Clement's ass.

Clement's hands dipped under Qaed's tank top, greedily skimming along the grooves of muscle lining his stomach. Qaed's chest stuttered under his touch, and Clement still couldn't quite believe he had this effect on him.

"We should take this somewhere," Qaed managed between hot, open-mouthed kisses. "Do you want to be in your room or mine?"

"Yours," Clement breathed. He wrenched himself away from Qaed, immediately missing the chill of his body against his, only for Qaed to grab his face and kiss him again. The kiss was all desperate tongue and teeth, and Clement melted against it. Maybe he could be okay with his first time being on the kitchen floor.

But Qaed pulled away finally, taking Clement by the hand and leading him to his bedroom. Qaed's room was smaller than Clement's; tidy, walls littered with movie posters. A bookshelf sat against the wall opposite his bed, action figures lining the top shelf. The shelves beneath were packed with books that Clement was pretty sure were graphic novels.

"I didn't know you were a comic book guy," Clement said as Qaed closed the door behind them. "And action figures?"

Qaed pressed his back against the door, a bashful smile playing at his lips. "Hey, you are the one who chose to come in here, not me. If you find all this unattractive–"

"I don't." In fact, Clement found Qaed even *more* attractive now. "I like hot, nerdy guys." A pause fell over them, Clement's eyes widening a fraction. *Shit.* He *did* like Qaed. A lot. More than he should like someone that he was using for novel fodder.

Maybe this was the wrong decision. The lines were getting muddied; he was never supposed to *feel* anything about this. And maybe it was wishful thinking, but the way Qaed was looking at Clement right now felt anything but meaningless. There was a heat in his eyes that made Clement shiver, one of the hands by his side flexing as if in anticipation. Clement couldn't wait to see what Qaed was about to do with that hand.

He wasn't strong enough to back out now. Every fiber of his body wanted this, wanted *Qaed.* Wanted to see all the parts of Qaed he tried so hard to hide.

Qaed closed the gap between them with two steps of his long legs, taking Clement's hand and guiding him towards the bed. "If this ends up not feeling right, you can say so whenever you want," he said, perching on the edge of the bed and pulling Clement by his belt loops to stand between his legs. "I will not be offended."

"I want this," he said, quietly but firmly. *I want you. Why can't you see that? What am I doing wrong?*

"Come here, then," Qaed said, and Clement was all too eager to do as he was told. He crawled into Qaed's bed, sinking back against the almost laughable amount of pillows at the head of Qaed's bed. Qaed slotted himself between the legs that Clement parted so readily for him. Clement sucked in a sharp breath, the anticipation of that strong thigh against him again making his entire body tremble. Qaed had hardly touched him yet and already, every nerve stood on end, waiting to be soothed by his hands, his tongue, whatever Qaed decided to touch him with.

The first thing that found Clement's bare skin were his hands, sliding up the hem of his t-shirt to skim over his stomach. He couldn't stop himself from whimpering, his back arching off the bed to help him tug his shirt off. Qaed sat back for a second, a move that would be torturous if it weren't for the hunger in the eyes that raked over Clement's bare torso.

"You can tell me what you want, Clement," Qaed murmured, neck craning down to plant hot kisses down his chest. "Tell me what feels good."

How could he when *everything* felt good? His brain short-circuited with every kiss, even more so the further down Qaed went. His mouth hovered over the waistband of Clement's pajama pants and he froze, immediately gripping Qaed's unbroken horn to stop him.

What he didn't expect was to be met with a groan. "Clem–" he gasped. "Is everything alright?"

So Qaed liked his horns being pulled. Noted. "Uh, d-don't go down there. I don't think I'm ready for that yet."

"Of course," Qaed said, pressing a kiss to the base of Clement's throat. *Fuck*, that was hot. The heat pulsing between his legs was almost unbearable, and it took everything in him not to beg for him. He couldn't even tell what it was that he wanted. The heat burning through his body was frying his brain.

Qaed adjusted his thigh to let it press against Clement's clothed cock, drawing a surprised moan from Clement. "Shit," he gasped, unable to stop himself from rocking his hips against Qaed's solid thigh. Qaed pressed against him in response, and Clement whimpered, balling his fists into the comforter beneath him.

"Gods, Clement, you look so good right now," Qaed said, his voice a low rumble that vibrated down Clement's entire body. Clement didn't know if the dirty talk was Qaed's way of enhancing the fantasy, but he didn't want it to stop. "Please, let me touch you."

"Yes, *please*," Clement begged, arching his back off the bed in greedy anticipation. Qaed ushered his pants down and Clement gave them a kick, letting them fall to the floor at the foot of the bed. The need ravaging through him clouded how vulnerable he felt right now, splayed out in front of Qaed in nothing but his boxers.

Qaed leaned in, his lips brushing against the shell of Clement's ear as his cold hand found Clement's cock. His hips snapped up against his touch, every nerve in his body alight. He'd always wondered what it would be like to have someone else's hand on him, and somehow, it was even better than he'd ever imagined. "So hard for me already," he breathed. "So impatient."

He *was.* Every move of Qaed's was agonizingly slow. Qaed's thick finger circled him tauntingly, and Clement whined, practically shoving his hips into his hand. "You like when I stroke your cock like that? Desperate boy." A soft groan filtered past his lips and directly into Clement's ear.

God, Clement didn't know dirty talk could be this good. "Yes, fuck, don't stop a single thing you're doing," he whimpered. "Can I touch you, too?"

"I have been imagining your hands on me since last night," Qaed said. "Please."

Clement maneuvered a hand between them to slip beneath Qaed's sweatpants. He wasn't wearing underwear. God bless this man. Both cocks greeted him at full attention, earning him a hiss from Qaed as he took one into his hand.

It looked mostly like a human cock, with the exception of hard ridges that trailed up the sides. Clement trailed the pad of his thumb along one of them, and Qaed's movements on Clement stopped briefly, his forehead coming to rest against Clement's chest. "Shit," he gasped, hips moving up into Clement's hand. He removed his hand from Qaed, who grunted in response, and pushed Qaed's sweatpants down.

Both dicks sprung free, their heads already leaking precum. The shafts were the same deep gray as the rest of Qaed, roped with vein-like ridges the same soft gray as his horns. Clement hadn't seen many dicks in his day, but he was pretty sure these were the most perfect ones he'd ever seen. They sat one on top of the other, with just one set of testicles beneath the bottom one.

His hand circled the base of the bottom one, and Qaed muffled his moans against Clement's lips. "Put one inside me, Qaed," Clement whispered into his mouth.

"Are you sure you are ready?"

Clement had never been more sure of anything in his life. He'd already resigned himself to the fact that it would probably hurt, but right now, it was all he wanted. All he needed. Hell, if he could manage to take both, he would. He needed to be filled to the brim with Qaed.

"Yes, please, I want you to fuck me," he breathed, lifting his hips up off the bed to push down his boxers. He kicked them off, and Qaed licked his lips like he was going to devour him.

God, did Clement hope he would.

"Just... go slow." Clement watched as Qaed lined himself up with Clement's dripping entrance, tipping his head back with a needy sigh as his head brushed against him.

He pushed only the head in and Clement hissed, pain blossoming through the lower half of his body. "Gods, you are so tight," Qaed groaned, pressing a hand against Clement's chest. Clement clutched it in an attempt to ground himself. "Are you okay?"

Clement let out a noncommittal sound. Maybe he'd been a little ambitious. "Your cock is bigger than I thought it was."

"I... am going to take that as a compliment," Qaed said, and Clement barked out a laugh past the pain.

After a minute or two of adjusting, the pain started to give way to pleasure, to the need for Qaed's cock buried to the hilt inside him. "Okay, I can take more," he said, angling his hips to more readily receive him.

Once he'd adjusted to Qaed's girth inside him, taking the rest of his cock was easy. His fists balled in the comforter beneath him as Qaed buried himself in him, hot tears gathering at the corners of his eyes. The pain hadn't completely subsided, but it was tolerable enough that it mingled with the rush of pleasure that came from the head of Qaed's cock hitting just the right spot inside him.

"Qaed, oh my God," Clement cried out. Once he had fully adjusted, he couldn't get enough. He shoved his hips up to meet Qaed's infuriatingly slow thrusts. "I need you. Please."

Qaed chuckled, looping his arms around Clement and pulling him into his arms. He sat back on his knees, Clement in his lap, so full of Qaed's glorious ribbed cock he was pretty sure he was seeing stars. Their new position allowed Clement to give Qaed's horns a sharp tug.

"Clement, you are driving me crazy," he gasped, pressing the bridge of his nose into the crook of Clement's neck. "Fuck, you take my cock so well."

Clement drew Qaed's head back by the horns, forcing their eyes to meet. Qaed was so... beautiful. A swell of emotion bubbled in the pit of Clement's stomach, mingling with the arousal that threatened to overflow. He could stay like this for hours and never grow tired of it.

"You wanna watch me cum on your dick?" he purred. He didn't recognize the version of himself he was when he was full of Qaed, but he liked it.

Qaed's eyes darkened and his soft, plump lips fell open. "Yes. Gods, yes, cum for me, Clem."

And he did. It wasn't like this was the first time Clement had ever orgasmed–he'd gotten pretty damn good at getting himself off over the years. But now, he wasn't sure he could ever go back. He wasn't sure he'd ever be able to cum again without Qaed's cock being involved.

His body was still trembling with the aftershocks of his orgasm when Qaed pulled out of him, taking both cocks into one large hand and giving them a few final strokes before he came. Even his cum was pretty–ropes of pearlescent blue coated Clement's chest, his stomach, and for a brief, filthy second, Clement wished he'd caught it in his mouth.

He collapsed back against the bed, but Qaed remained seated, revering him with a look that Clement couldn't quite place. He reached for Qaed's arm, tugging him down to his level. Qaed laughed breathily, falling to Clement's side. "Are you certain that was your first time? Or was that just an excuse to get me into bed? Because you were... incredible."

Clement's cheeks warmed under the praise. "I could get you into bed without lying to you," he grinned. He turned to look at Qaed, the tenderness in his eyes making Clement's stomach swoop. "Thank you."

Qaed chuckled quietly, pushing a lock of sweat-soaked hair out of Clement's eyes. "I would say that I would be delighted to do it again, but I suppose you only get one first time."

Right. This was always meant to be a one-time thing. Clement swallowed, trying to ignore the disappointment rising in the pit of his stomach. "Well, if I get amnesia and forget that I've ever had sex, I'll make sure to come back to you so we can do this again."

"But then how will you remember to ask me?"

"I'll leave a note to myself–'Clement, if you ever develop amnesia and forget the first time you had sex, go to Qaed. He's pretty decent in bed.'"

"You were making some sounds that told me I was a little more than pretty decent." Qaed smirked.

Qaed was so much more than pretty decent, Clement wasn't sure he'd ever have better. He took a pillow from the other side of the bed and buried his face in it. "Shut up. Forget you ever heard any of those sounds."

"That will be hard to do." Qaed pulled the pillow from Clement's face. "As hot as you look right now... you are more than welcome to use my bathroom to clean up."

Clement's cheeks flushed. "Right. Yeah. Should probably do that." He sat up, and his first instinct was to pull Qaed in for a kiss.

But they hadn't agreed on that. The sex was where it ended. Where it *needed* to end. He couldn't use Qaed for this anymore. He shoved himself out of Qaed's bed and into the bathroom, and the second the door closed behind him, tears sprung to his eyes.

God, what had he done?

Dholzi undid the bandages binding Vandu's chest, and she shrunk before him, wrapping her arms around herself. He gently pried her arms apart, taking all of her in. Desire flashed in his eyes as he shoved her back against the bedroll. "Gods, you're beautiful," he murmured, slotting his thigh between her legs. She fell apart easily for him and his hands trailed down the length of her torso slowly, reverently. There was no hiding herself in front of Dholzi now. He had no choice but to know her. All of her. And that was just as terrifying as it was exhilarating.

– Excerpt from *To Spite a Raven's Heart* by Clement Hall

Chapter Thirteen

Qaed

WAKING UP WITHOUT CLEMENT next to him felt just as weird as expecting him to be there.

Qaed wasn't generally in the habit of spending more time with the men he slept with than he absolutely had to. He'd fall asleep in their beds, but the second he woke up, whether it was late in the morning or before the sun rose, he'd make his way home. Sometimes he'd leave a message. Most times he wouldn't.

He would've left a note for Clement, though. Or maybe he would've stuck around to hear the sleep in his voice, to see the drool crusted at the corner of his mouth that he'd vehemently try to deny.

Instead, he was stuck in his own bed, alone, with two erections stuffed into his shorts; the byproduct of a particularly vivid dream involving the man that had been in his bed last night. He shoved himself out of bed with a groan, the seam of his boxers rubbing against his throbbing cocks. If this was what every morning was going to be like after having a single night's taste of being with Clement, he was well and truly fucked.

Hells, he'd been on the path to being fucked for a long time. Clement was the first thing on his mind when he woke up and had been the last thing on it before he fell asleep. He was so addicted to this man, he couldn't even escape him in his dreams.

But Clement had been abundantly clear what he was after—and it wasn't this. He'd let Qaed fuck him so he could say he had. And Qaed had no right to be upset about that because he'd agreed to it.

He went into the bathroom and splashed hot water on his face, the shock startling him awake and taming the boners straining against his underwear. Once he deemed himself calm enough to leave the room, he dressed in a pair of dark jeans and a black t-shirt and headed for the kitchen.

Unsurprisingly, Clement had beaten Qaed to it. But he wasn't making coffee, like Qaed would have expected. He was unpacking a shipping canister on the counter, pulling out jars, cans, and bags with colorful branding. He was in the same pajamas as he had been last night, which threatened to get Qaed riled up again. Maybe he should've stayed in his bedroom longer.

"What is all that?" he asked, peering over Clement's shoulder. Being close to him felt so normal now; even the normally jumpy Clement didn't seem to mind having Qaed inches away from him.

"Cecily sent me a package of Earth stuff," Clement grinned over his shoulder. "God, I haven't seen this stuff in months. *Pancake* mix?" He clutched a narrow, rectangular box to his chest. He spotted something else in the shipping box, drawing an excited gasp from him. "English breakfast tea!"

"Cecily is your sister, right?" he asked, moving to Clement's side and taking a bag from the counter. It felt like it was just full of air, but something rattled around in it. The words 'salt and vinegar potato chips' were emblazoned across the front.

Clement placed the box of pancake mix on the counter in favor of reaching into the shipping container. "I'm surprised you remembered that," he said, but his tone wasn't teasing. His voice was soft, and it made Qaed want to push back the feathery hair that had fallen into his face.

"She is the only person you ever talk about aside from Candy." Qaed reached into the box at the same time as Clement, his fingertips brushing over the back of Clement's hand. But Clement didn't pull away. Instead, he took the blue plastic-wrapped box they were both reaching for and peeled back the plastic protecting the top of it. Little brown discs were arranged in three perfectly straight rows, a strong smell of something Qaed didn't recognize emanating from them.

"Yeah, I guess that's a solid point." Clement pulled one of the round things from the container and popped it into his mouth. Qaed hadn't expected it to crunch quite as loudly as it did. He let out a soft moan, one that made Qaed's breath hitch in the back of his throat. "Oh my God, I missed Oreos so much. You gotta try one."

Qaed took one, giving it a cautionary sniff. "What *is* this?"

Clement shushed him. "Just try it!"

So he did. He took a small bite, his mouth immediately flooded with sweetness and something that almost tasted like the coffee Clement made. His jaw stilled mid-bite as he assessed whether or not he wanted to keep chewing. Clement watched him, pulling the two discs apart and licking out the white filling.

Now he *definitely* couldn't keep chewing. He swallowed, though he wasn't entirely sure he wanted to venture another bite. "That was... interesting."

"You don't like it?" Clement almost looked personally offended. He stared into the package longingly and Qaed could practically hear him considering another one.

He offered his half-eaten one to Clement. "It does not taste like food," Qaed said with a slight wrinkle of his nose.

"Yeah... it's probably *barely* food. American food is dangerous." Clement took the strange thing from Qaed's hand and stuck it into his mouth. "I was gonna offer to make you breakfast like what I eat at home, but I don't know how much you'll like it."

"If it is anything like whatever I just ate... you are probably right." Qaed grinned, and Clement rolled his eyes. "But I would like to try it anyway, if you want to make it."

"I was gonna make it whether you said yes or not. After four months of eating *your* food, a morning of Earth food won't kill you," Clement said, bumping Qaed with his hip to reach the cabinet in front of him. Qaed was pretty sure a morning of Earth food *might* kill him, but he'd do it. For Clement. Maybe falling in love *was* a bad thing.

He focused all of his attention on the rest of the boxes and bags Clement pulled out of the shipping container so as not to dwell on the fact that he was absolutely, without a doubt, falling in love with this man. He'd eat this chemical-laden, mysteriously colored food every day for the rest of his life if it was what Clement wanted.

Once Clement emptied the container, Qaed took it from the counter and stuck it outside their front door to be picked up. "So, what are you going to make?" he asked once he was back in the kitchen.

"I was thinking about pancakes... we'd normally have bacon and eggs too, but they wouldn't have survived the journey out here. And we *have* to have tea. Candy's dad used to make it for me all the time because I was the only one who would ever drink it with him." Clement filled his kettle with water, and Qaed took down two mugs from the cabinet. He truthfully hadn't had much use for mugs during much of the time he'd lived in this apartment. They'd been pristinely white since he got them. But now, the insides were stained brown, a discoloration that wouldn't come off no matter how hard he'd scrubbed when he first noticed it happening.

But he'd stopped trying to scrub them away in the past few weeks, the reminders of his four months of mornings with Clement, drinking coffee that Qaed was slowly starting to like and talking about everything and nothing. He hoped he'd never have perfectly white mugs ever again.

Clement placed small bags of what looked like leaves into the mugs and poured hot water over them. The smell was nothing like coffee; it actually reminded him a lot of *qolqi*, a medicinal drink the Alqen elders made when the children were sick. A pang of homesickness stirred in him, one that he hadn't felt in a long time.

Qaed watched Clement as he dumped some of the contents of a box into a mixing bowl and added water. The white powder turned to a thick slop that Qaed thought looked wholly unappetizing, but he stood back, letting Clement work. He poured the mixture into a pan on the stove. "When Candy's dad used to make pancakes for us when we were little, he'd take requests for what shapes we wanted ours to be. Candy always wanted hers in the shape of hearts or Mickey Mouse, and I was always too afraid to ask for anything because I didn't wanna make things harder for him. And now I kind of wish I'd taken him up on it, because his always used to look *so pretty* and this looks nothing like a heart."

Qaed peered into the pan at the lumpy blob of white. "It certainly does not," he said. "Maybe... an anatomically correct heart?"

"If that's what your heart looked like, I'd be worried about you." He slotted the spatula under the blob and flipped it, revealing a caramelized brown surface.

Qaed leaned back against the counter next to the stove, his arms over his chest. "I did not know you had known Candy for that long."

"Yep. Best friends since we were babies. Thank God, too. I don't know what I would've done without her and her family." Clement stared into the pan for a moment, a wistful smile touching his lips. "They're really cool people. I wouldn't be half the man I am now if I hadn't known them. Her dad especially taught me a lot when I first came out."

"Came out?"

Clement froze, as if he'd said something he wasn't supposed to. But his shoulders relaxed after a second. "Yeah. I came out as trans when I was nineteen. My mom wasn't the most accepting of it, but the Murdocks were. They threw me a party and gave me all kinds of gift cards to buy new clothes."

Qaed had a feeling he wasn't understanding a very important piece of this. "I am sorry, but I have never heard the term *trans* before," he said, giving the goo in the mixing bowl an idle mix.

Clement exhaled slowly. "I don't know how gender works with your species, but with humans, we're assigned one when we're born depending on what our bodies look like. And I was supposed to be a girl." He picked up the thing in the pan–ah, *pancake* made sense now–and set it on a plate. He went to pour more of the batter into the pan but Qaed stopped him, taking it from his hands.

"That is a strange thing to put on a child," Qaed said quietly, focusing all of his energy on pouring the batter into as close a shape to a heart as he could. "Qintaril are not given a gender at birth. It is chosen when the child is old enough to form an opinion. Sometimes it takes a while, and sometimes it changes, but it is not something we force on anyone."

Clement let out a sardonic laugh. "My life would've been so much easier if that was the case. I was telling my mom I was a boy from the moment I was old enough to talk."

Qaed put the bowl down on the counter, looking over at a suddenly pensive Clement. All he wanted to do was pull him into his arms as if to apologize to little Clement, the child who felt like he had no support in the world. "I cannot imagine how difficult that was."

"Honestly, the hardest part was all of the medical stuff. I had surgery to reduce my chest and I *still* can't feel it." Clement gave his chest a pat with both hands. "And then there's the weekly testosterone shots. I wanted to get bottom surgery before I came out here but it's just too expensive." He clasped both hands over Qaed's to help him flip the pancake, and Qaed could have sworn that his heart stopped for a second. "Turns out there's a species of alien out here in Kratos hogging all the dicks. Why do *you* need *two?*"

Qaed tipped his head back and laughed. "Not all of us have two. I am just one of the lucky ones. I would say I would give you one, but... having two is kind of fantastic."

Clement moved to Qaed's side to pluck the bags of leaves out of their mugs. "You already gave me one. Last night," he winked, and Qaed's mouth fell open. Honestly, he'd had every intention of pretending like this hadn't happened. That was what he thought Clement wanted.

"Of course. You could not have handled both," Qaed grinned despite the rushing of his heart in his ears.

Clement blanched, snatching the spatula from him. "I totally could've!"

Wanna bet? He wanted *so* badly to drag him back to his bedroom and challenge that notion, to bend him over and see both of his cocks disappear into Clement's two pretty little holes. He shoved the thought out of his mind as quickly as he could. If he got even remotely hard, it'd be damn near impossible to miss in these jeans. "Whatever you say," he mused instead, watching Clement slide the slightly more heart-shaped second pancake onto the plate.

Together, they made a hearty stack of pancakes and took them to the dining table with a jug of some sort of amber liquid and their two mugs of tea. Qaed took a sip of his tea; with the couple of spoonfuls of sugar Clement had added to it, it was much more pleasant than the coffee.

"Okay, so this is maple syrup," Clement said, lifting the jug of liquid. "Well, it's not, really. It's maple *flavored* syrup. This is the cheap stuff my mom used to buy." He poured a hearty glug of it over their pancakes, the thick syrup seeping into the fluffy pancakes and pooling on the plate beneath them. "Just a warning, this stuff's sweet."

"I am starting to wonder how you humans survive on all of this sugar," Qaed said, approaching the pancakes with a cautious fork. "I think eating this as my first meal of the day might kill me."

"Don't be so dramatic." As if to make a point, Clement cut off a piece of pancake dripping in syrup and stuck it in his mouth. "Oh my God, this is so good," he said, leaning his head back and closing his eyes. "It tastes like home."

Qaed's stomach suddenly felt like lead. It couldn't have been easy for Clement to come out here alone without so much as the comfort foods he grew up with. And

Qaed wasn't exactly the most steadfast person to be his anchor. "You must miss Earth a lot," he said, taking a small bite of pancake. Much better than the strange brown thing Clement had offered him earlier, though it tasted mostly of chemicals. His stomach started to ache after the second bite.

"Weirdly enough, I don't. I miss some of the things that I grew up with. I miss snow. I miss... walking around Brooklyn and stopping for a slice of pizza, or going to a new restaurant that opened just a few days ago because there's *always* one of those in New York." He trailed his fork through the pool of syrup on the plate. "But I don't miss my life back there. I feel free out here."

"I know what you mean." Qaed busied himself with cutting the pancake into little triangles, but didn't venture to eat another one. "I moved out here to Veterok-III a few years ago now, with Votra. I love Alqen, my planet. But living the life I live now is much easier here."

"Was your life really different on Alqen?" Clement asked.

"Very." Qaed put his fork down, his appetite officially gone. "I was a bounty hunter when I lived on Alqen, as many qintaril are." A lump formed at the back of his throat, the sticky syrup only serving to glue it there. "But that was a lifetime ago. Now, I live here where all of my friends are. And I actually have time to see them."

"And you have time to let your weird roommate make you eat weird Earth food," Clement said with a laugh.

"And to let him make me take him out on fake dates," Qaed added, counting off his list on his fingers, "...and to let him get me addicted to caffeine." *And to let him make me fall in love with him.*

"Damn, now that you say that, I sound like a really shitty roommate," Clement snorted, leaning back in his chair. "Did you at least *like* the pancakes?"

"Will it make you feel more like a shitty roommate if I say no?"

"Yes!" Clement whined, pulling the plate away from Qaed.

"...Then yes, I liked them." Qaed made a point of shoving another piece into his mouth and immediately regretted it. It was no wonder humans had such short life spans. He took a sip of warm, slightly bitter tea, which was much needed after what felt like three bites of nothing but sugar.

Clement rested his chin in his palm, those warm brown eyes settling on Qaed like hot stones. "Thanks for lying to me to make me feel better."

"Any time."

Chapter Fourteen

Clement

THE MONTHS LEADING UP to the convention passed in a blur of Clement really struggling to edit the words that had once flown out of him so easily. Since that night with Qaed, there'd been a solid block in his mind, one that he couldn't get over no matter how hard he tried.

But the book was passable. He wouldn't be showing it in its entirety to the agents yet, anyway. He just had to prepare a pitch and get himself ready for the mortifying ordeal of agent speed dating. It still didn't feel entirely real that he was going in the first place.

The flight over was long–the conference was still on Veterok-III, but on the opposite side of it. Shuttles were much faster than Earth's planes, but it still took the better half of a day to get there. Clement couldn't sit still the entire flight over.

And that didn't change once they arrived. Qaed insisted on carrying all of their luggage in–normally, Clement would have argued, but he was too busy taking in the sights. The Grand Dyrbov was massive, apparently one of the biggest on the entire planet. The lobby was blindingly gold, with shiny floors Clement felt bad for stepping on in his scuffed sneakers. Gilded Roman pillars framed the receptionist desk.

The concierge at the front desk made a big show of taking their luggage from Qaed, promising to deliver it to their room safely. That was another thing Clement wasn't entirely prepared for. Despite the fact that they'd be in separate beds, the thought of sleeping in the same room as him made his heart race.

Their room was on the thirteenth floor; Clement had never been a superstitious person, but his mom was. She would've told him to book a different room. And for a moment, he considered it.

Until Qaed came to a stop beside him in the long hallway of the hotel's thirteenth floor. "Overwhelmed?" he asked, placing a reassuring hand on his shoulder.

God, he was. He felt like he shouldn't be here, like he was playing pretend. The agents were going to laugh him off tomorrow. "A little," he said quietly.

"Good. That means you care." Qaed squeezed his shoulder and started off down the hallway, leaving Clement with little choice but to follow him.

Their room was about halfway down the hallway—Room 1313. His mom was *rolling* in her grave. Qaed tapped his comm to the keypad and opened the door for Clement.

The room was a modest size, the window wall on the opposite side making the room feel bigger. Pressed against the wall was one bed—a large one, at least a queen size—with more pillows than anyone could ever need and a plush, crushed velvet comforter the color of rubies.

Clement blinked. He'd *definitely* booked a double room... right? Qaed didn't seem terribly bothered, immediately flopping down on the bed face-first and letting out the sigh he'd probably been holding in all morning.

"Don't get too comfortable," Clement grumbled. "I need to go down there and fix this. There were supposed to be two beds."

"Ah. And here I thought you were trying to hint at something," Qaed said, rolling onto his back with a grunt. "Gods, this bed is comfortable."

Clement snorted, crossing the room to sit on the bed. Shit, it *was* comfortable. The mattress was just soft enough that he sunk into it when he sat, and he almost gave in to laying down as well. "Holy shit."

"Mm-hm," Qaed murmured, and when Clement looked down at him, his eyes were closed.

Clement couldn't help but smile. He looked so peaceful, his cheek adorably mashed into the comforter. Moving him would just be wrong.

"Qaed. Don't you wanna nap in your own bed?"

"My own bed is hours away. This one is fine." Qaed's voice was growing heavy with sleep, and Clement clicked his tongue.

"You know what I meant." But if Qaed wasn't moving... maybe Clement didn't need to, either. "...Can I lay next to you?"

Qaed made a little noise that Clement couldn't decipher, but he rolled over a few inches to give Clement room. He kicked his shoes off and shifted to lay next to Qaed—not too close, but close enough that he could make out every detail of Qaed's face. His deep gray skin was smooth, marred with a smattering of small scars he'd never really noticed before. He fought the urge to trail his fingertips along the crest of his cheekbone.

Qaed let out a tiny grunt, his lips pursing briefly. *He's asleep.* He'd never understood the appeal of watching your partner sleep. Clement felt like he was at his ugliest when he slept. He snored, he flailed his limbs about like a drunken octopus. And he drooled. A lot.

But Qaed looked so calm, it made Clement's chest ache. He deserved this peace. Clement gave in to his urges, skimming the pad of his pointer finger along the soft slopes of Qaed's face. The sheath of hard tissue that made up the bridge of his nose was still smooth under Clement's touch, culminating in the cutest nose tip he'd ever seen.

God, what was he doing? He'd paraded Qaed around like a toy for the last four months then dragged him across the planet, only to get them a hotel room where Qaed didn't even have his own bed.

He was *really,* really bad at all this. And Qaed deserved better. Once all this was over, he was going to leave Qaed alone. No more dragging him into fake dates because Clement wasn't creative enough to come up with them on his own.

"Thank you for everything, Qaed," he whispered, leaning in and pressing the lightest of kisses to Qaed's cheek. He let himself curl in closer to Qaed than he probably should and let his eyes flutter closed.

Clement woke up what felt like hours later with a solid arm draped across him, a horn dangerously close to his eye. At least his glasses would've protected him from being impaled through the eyeball. He ducked his head, shifting down slightly to remove himself from danger.

He pressed his face into Qaed's chest, breathing him in. He didn't smell of woodsy, spicy cologne like he normally did. He just smelled like... Qaed. And Clement kind of liked that better.

Qaed let out a sleepy grumble, shifting a little over Clement but not withdrawing his arm. Clement didn't want him to. "Shit, what time is it?" he asked, words slurring together with sleep.

Clement squinted against the screen of his comm. "Almost eight," he said, rolling over to lay on his back. Qaed's arm remained across his stomach, and Clement placed a hand on top of it. "We should probably get some food."

"Or we could just keep sleeping." Clement turned his head to look at Qaed, whose eyes were still very much closed. *God,* he was cute.

"We haven't eaten since before we got here. I know you're hungry," Clement said, sitting up and begrudgingly pulling himself out of Qaed's grip. "*I* am, so if you don't get up, I'm gonna go eat without you."

"You will not," Qaed said, opening his eyes blearily. He rubbed at them, stifling a yawn. "Alright, alright, I will go with you." He stared up at Clement, a sleepy smile pulling at his lips, and Clement was overcome with the urge to lean down and kiss him.

They ventured into the hallway and back down to the lobby. It seemed like most of the conference's guests had the same idea to arrive the night before. Groups of three to four people dotted the lobby, and Clement sucked in a breath. Shit, should he be socializing already? He was pretty sure he had aggressive bags under his eyes, and he wasn't dressed for the occasion in his old anime t-shirt and jeans that were half a size too big.

He shouldn't be here in the first place. "I lied, I wanna go back upstairs," Clement said quickly, placing a hand on Qaed's chest. "I'm not that hungry after all."

"Wait, what is wrong?" Qaed asked, looking down at Clement with narrowed eyes. "I think there is a restaurant just on the other side of the lobby–"

That would mean he'd have to walk through these people, these professional writers, and they'd look him up and down and wonder if he was lost. And maybe he was. "We can just order room service!" Clement said, turning tail and heading back for the elevator before Qaed could stop him.

Qaed caught up to him in a few long strides. "Clement." Clement's heart pounded in his ears, a sound that only grew louder when Qaed grabbed his hand. "What happened just now?"

Irritated tears stung at his eyes. He was nervous, more nervous than he knew how to handle, and the most frustrating part of it all was that he didn't want Qaed to see him like this. He jabbed the up button to call the elevator.

"Clement," Qaed tried again, and Clement didn't dare answer him until the doors closed behind them.

"Fuck," Clement breathed, whipping off his glasses and wiping his eyes. Through his blurred vision, he could barely make out Qaed pressing something on the elevator's control panel, and the elevator jerked to a halt. "I thought I was ready for this. But then I saw all those people down there and I–" He hiccupped. "This is really scary."

"I can only imagine." Qaed's hands circled around Clement's upper arms. "But you are incredible, alright? Someone is going to adore you and your book."

"That's easy for you to say. You haven't read it."

"Then let me," Qaed said, and Clement shrunk under the intensity of his stare. "I will read it tonight."

The thought of Qaed reading his book made him want to fall through the bottom of this elevator. So much of this book was just... him. His crooked smile, his nerdy hobbies, how good he was at cooking. How kind his eyes were, how soft his touch was despite how physically strong he was.

"Okay," Clement found himself saying, despite everything in him telling him not to. "You sure you wanna read the whole thing tonight?"

"Sure. We will order room service, you can rest... and I will read your entire book."

Clement wanted to kiss this stupid, sweet man. "Thank you," he said quietly, and much to his chagrin, Qaed dropped his hands from his arms.

The elevator dinged as it deposited them on the thirteenth floor, and the moment they found themselves back in their room, he relaxed. He could worry about the people downstairs tomorrow. For now, his only audience was Qaed.

The man he'd written this entire fucking book about. He collapsed onto the bed with a groan, the embarrassment of his tears finally sinking in. "I'm sorry about all that."

"Hey, give me some room, too," Qaed said, giving Clement's thigh a swat. Clement rolled over a few inches and Qaed sat cross-legged next to him. "You have nothing to apologize for. You have been getting ready for this for a long time now. It must be terrifying."

"It is. You think I can send, like, a hologram version of me down there to do the event? I could just control it from up here, then I don't have to actually *see* anyone."

"I heard someone tried that at an entrepreneurial conference once. He got banned from ever attending a conference again because the hologram malfunctioned and instead of being a hologram of the guy, it was just a hologram of his ass."

Clement sat straight up, gaping. "No way."

"Wow, I actually did not think you would fall for that one," Qaed said, and Clement whacked him with a pillow.

"Ass." He rolled to the opposite side of the bed and reached into his suitcase for his laptop. "Is there a room service menu in here?"

"Way ahead of you." Qaed waved a small datapad at Clement.

"Order whatever you want. Just get enough for both of us," Clement said as he sat up, logging into his computer. His novel document stared back at him; he hadn't opened it in at least a week now. He gave it a cursory scroll, in case there were any glaring spelling or grammar issues. He wanted Qaed to think it was perfect.

"You have given me too much power. But I will use it responsibly," Qaed said sagely, and Clement rolled his eyes. *Cute.*

He shoved his laptop into Qaed's lap before he could change his mind. "Well, when you're done, there's my book. If you've changed your mind about reading it, though—"

"I have not." Qaed passed Clement the menu datapad, showing him that the order was placed. He balanced the laptop between his crossed legs and scooted back against the cushions. "Alright, now do not bother me until the food gets here. I have something important to do."

Clement laughed, laying back into the mattress. This was fine. Totally fine. He'd be *totally* normal about Qaed reading his book. "I hope you like it," he said. He *needed* him to.

Chapter Fifteen

Qaed

QAED DIDN'T READ MUCH. He loved comic books, but they hardly required any reading. He couldn't remember the last time he'd read a proper book.

But he couldn't stop reading from the moment he started. He felt like Clement had served him his heart on a platter, and he had every intention of committing every word into his own.

He let his hands rest on the edges of the laptop, wondering just how much time in Clement's life he'd spent hunched over this thing. A small, worn-out sticker clung stubbornly to the bottom corner under the keyboard, and Qaed found himself toying with it as he read.

The book's premise excited him immediately; a young orlix named Vandu disguising herself as her brother Straal to prevent him from enlisting in a war that might kill him. He found himself getting lost in the world Clement had created, dissecting every sentence as if it might unlock something about Clement he didn't already know.

Room service's knock at the door startled him out of his reading, and Clement jumped up from the bed. "I got it," he said, patting Qaed's knee and opening the door. He heard a small exclamation of "holy shit," followed by profuse apologies and thanks.

"Qaed, did you have to order the entire kitchen?" Clement blanched as he wheeled in a trolley of metal cloches.

"Trust me, there was so much more on the menu that I wanted to try." Qaed set the laptop on the bed and moved to the edge of it. "I have an entire book to read. I need the energy."

Clement flushed, opening one of the cloches to reveal a platter of golden, fried sticks of something. "Oh my God," he gasped. "Are these french fries?"

Qaed shrugged. "Maybe?" He genuinely couldn't remember the name of anything. He'd just gone down the list of foods under the Earth header and ordered it all.

Clement took one and immediately grinned. "Yep. French fry." He held one out to Qaed and he took it into his mouth. Surprisingly, it was delicious—crispy and salty.

"Oh. I like that," he said. He plucked another from the plate and reclaimed his position on the bed, laptop in his lap. "What else is there?" He returned to the book as Clement opened the rest of the containers of food. His little gasps of excitement crescendoed, the last one he opened eliciting the loudest gasp of all.

"This is a really weird mix of food, but I don't even care. There's *egg rolls* here!" The mattress depressed beside him as Clement jumped onto it, throwing his arms around Qaed. "Thank you. I really needed this tonight."

Qaed squeezed Clement's forearm, warming under his touch. "I thought it might cheer you up," he said. "Can you pass me some more of those french fries?"

Clement made up a plate of fries and passed them to Qaed, who balanced the plate on his upper leg. He could eat a dangerous amount of these things. He popped a few more into his mouth while Clement busied himself with making a plate.

"I can't say I've ever had pizza and gyoza in the same meal before, but I'm not complaining," he said, sitting cross-legged beside Qaed. His whole face seemed brighter now, after everything that happened in the elevator.

"How does it compare to how it normally tastes on Earth?" Qaed asked.

"Well, the pizza kind of tastes like what I used to get at school when I was a kid, which isn't the worst, I guess. But these gyoza are pretty amazing." He flipped on the television and settled in, his side pressed against Qaed's.

As Qaed continued reading, Clement plied him with Earth dish after Earth dish. The french fries were still his favorite, though the silky, ambiguously named 'Earth dessert' came in close second. Clement had called it 'flan,' which, to him, was just as ambiguous.

Before long, even his favorite french fries went cold and forgotten beside him as he became engrossed in the book. Qaed rested a hand at the base of his throat as he reached the culmination of Vandu and Dholzi's relationship. His heartbeat drummed against the thumb resting at the side of his neck. Tears welled in his eyes as Vandu confessed her feelings for Dholzi, and they shared a long, lingering kiss under a meteor storm.

"I can't lose you, Dholzi," Vandu whispered, *Vaessoth's icy winds whipping her hair about her face. "Because of you... I only just started to understand myself. Who I am. I don't know who I am without you."*

Dholzi grimaced, clutching at the bandages around his ribs. Vandu rested her hands on top of his, as if she might make even a little bit of difference. "You'll be fine without me, Van. You're powerful, resilient, stubborn as the hells...." He laughed, the sound cut off by a low groan of pain. His visage blurred with her tears, and she shifted her hands to cup his face. "You've never needed me."

"I've always needed you, idiot." Hot tears stung Vandu's cheeks. "I still need you. You're not allowed to die."

"If I do, at least I'll die having met you." Dholzi lifted a hand to rest on her cheek, and she turned her head to kiss his palm. "Pretty sure my life couldn't get any better than this."

"Guess you better live to find out." Vandu kissed him carefully as if she might break him, his own tears warm against her thumbs.

Qaed cleared his throat, one stubborn tear rolling down his cheek. He wasn't sure he'd ever felt quite so understood in his life. Dholzi was *him,* immortalized on page, in text that Clement had labored over for months.

Clement deserved a confession under a meteor storm, not in a hotel room, surrounded by vague approximations of Earth food. "I am going to get some fresh air," he said, placing the laptop on the bed next to him. He stood, offering a hand to Clement. "Come with me?"

Clement grinned. "What, you bored of the book already?"

"Quite the opposite," Qaed said as Clement took his hand to stand up. He opened the door to the balcony and let Clement step out first before he followed.

The night air was chillier here than at home, which he appreciated but Clement immediately shivered against.

This hemisphere was also home to a different moon, a giant, pale blue moon with a visibly craggy surface. It took up most of the night sky, casting a milky glow across the street beneath them. The district was mostly silent now, save for a few shuttles speeding by.

"So... you like the book so far?" Clement asked, leaning his arms against the balcony's railing.

Qaed leaned against the steel railing, his back to the sky. The view from here was much better than anything he'd see out there. "Clement, the book is incredible. Except for Dholzi. He can be a bit...."

"Frustrating? Thick-headed?"

"I was going to say *annoyingly handsome.*" Qaed smirked. "He reminds me of someone."

"He's supposed to. I didn't drag you into all this research for nothing." Clement laced his fingers together, focusing his gaze on them. "He *is* frustrating, because he doesn't realize how incredible of a person he is. He puts himself down when he thinks other people won't notice and plays it off as a joke. But he's funny. Sweet. The most genuinely kind person I— Vandu's ever met."

Qaed's stomach swooped uncomfortably, and he steadied himself with both hands on the rail. "But he knows that he does not deserve Vandu. He knows that Vandu could have anyone she wants. And Dholzi is just some guy who was lucky enough to cross paths with her."

Clement scoffed. "Trust me, Vandu couldn't have any guy she wants. Vandu's a mess. She's so busy doing everything everyone else wants from her that she basically has no idea who *she* is, what *she* wants out of life. And Dholzi just... happens to be the first person to make her want something, to make her want to *be* something instead of letting everyone else around her dictate her life."

Qaed placed a hand on one of Clement's arms. "I am certain that Dholzi would be more than honored to be a part of whatever it is Vandu wants with her life, whether that be following the life of a soldier or... a writer." Clement's head snapped up, his glittering eyes meeting Qaed's.

"Yeah? What makes you think that?" Clement asked, his voice a hair above a whisper.

"I think I understand Dholzi quite well." Qaed smiled, brushing his thumb through the dusting of dark hair atop Clement's arm. "As a fellow annoyingly handsome man–"

Clement let out a long groan. "I knew I shouldn't have modeled a character after you. It *would* go right to your head." But he laughed, leaning his head against

Qaed's shoulder. Qaed could smell his sweet, floral shampoo, and he thought for a second about burying his nose in his hair. "Vandu doesn't feel... good enough for Dholzi. Vandu should probably get her own shit together before she even entertains a relationship with Dholzi."

Qaed gave into his impulses, resting his cheek atop Clement's head. "Vandu moved to a new galaxy and wrote a book in the span of four months. I think that can count as *having her shit together.*"

Clement let out a quiet laugh. "You just gave up on the whole metaphor thing, huh?"

"It was getting difficult, I will admit."

"It kind of was." Clement fell quiet for a moment. "I dunno. I feel like I'm just getting to know myself. I remember so little of my twenties–it's all just a blur of work and dealing with my overbearing mom... and then *taking care* of her. Her discovering she had Crohn's, getting colon cancer, and dying all happened in the course of five years. The me that existed before doesn't feel like a real person anymore, and I don't know who the guy on the other side of it is. How can I be right for anyone when I don't know who I am?"

Sorrow twisted in the center of Qaed's chest. "Unfortunately, I understand exactly how that feels." He was grateful that Clement was facing away from him in this very moment. "Two years ago, I nearly died. Got shot in the chest during a mission for work."

"That's what your scar's from," Clement said quietly, more like a statement than a question.

"Yes. The phaser beam went directly through my heart, and they had to go in and repair the hole. I still do not know how... or why I survived." Qaed's throat tightened. This was the first time he'd spoken about it out loud. Everyone else in his life had been there when it happened, and even despite them witnessing it, Qaed hadn't had the strength to talk about it.

Clement tensed next to him. "The recovery took a full year, and I cannot remember a second of it. And then I hardly remember the year after it because I drank every time I thought about the fact that I nearly died." Qaed steeled his jaw against the wave of tears prickling his sinuses. "I do not know who I am either. But I am quite certain I know exactly who you are."

"You think so?" Clement asked quietly. Qaed could feel the damp spot growing on his shoulder, and he couldn't bring himself to care.

"I do." Qaed sniffed, the tears dangerously close to winning. "You are... a man with immense talent. You have such an incredible way with words, which I never would have believed before I read your book, considering you use most of your words out loud to bully me." Clement let out a thick laugh, once again taking his glasses off and wiping his eyes. "You find so much beauty in everything. When we do new things together, I cannot even bring myself to look at what is going on around us because the joy in your eyes is... breathtaking."

"Qaed–"

"You are someone who has come out on the other side of having *so* much thrown at him, and somehow, you are still so unshakably kind. I do not know how you do it."

Clement pulled away from Qaed, and for a second, his heart dropped. But Clement shifted to position himself between Qaed's legs, sliding his arms around his middle. "And you are the man with the biggest heart I have ever met, who treats everyone who steps into his life even for a second like a member of his family. You can throw together a meal with the most random of ingredients and it'll taste like a professional chef made it. You're so strong, so disciplined, but so gentle. But, to be fair, you also bully me a pretty decent amount." He flashed Qaed those adorable teeth and it took every ounce of his self control not to kiss him.

"Your bar for professional chef-dom must be quite low," Qaed murmured, taking Clement's face in both of his hands and brushing the tears from the corners of his eyes.

"Actually, I'm *really* pretentious about food. I thought you would have known that by now."

"I never would have guessed after trying the Earth food you were *so* excited to have back."

"You know, a lot of people would consider not liking Oreos to be a red flag. You're lucky I'm not one of those people." Clement clasped Qaed's larger hands in his. "And for the record... I'm glad you're here. I don't wanna think about what my life might have been like if I hadn't met you."

Qaed wished he could burn this image of Clement into his mind forever, his pink-dusted cheeks bathed in moonlight, stars twinkling in his eyes. His lower lip wobbled despite his best efforts to stop it. "How does the book end, Clement?" he whispered.

Clement turned his face to the side slightly, brushing his lips across the part of Qaed's palm he could reach. "Vandu and Dholzi live happily ever after. It's a romance. They always have to end up together."

"Do they?" The tears rolled freely down Qaed's cheeks now, whether he wanted them to or not. "Do you think... do you think that rule extends to real life, too?"

"We followed all the rules. We started out as roommates, we fake dated. We even got only-one-bedded," Clement laughed. This time, it was his turn to wipe Qaed's tears away.

"Ah, so us not having separate beds was your fault. Just another part of your scheme," Qaed said. But this felt real. It had to be. Because if it wasn't... he wasn't sure he'd ever be able to trust his own heart again.

"No, that one was a lucky accident." Clement leaned in, his nose brushing Qaed's. "And now, we're having our big confession scene, where the main character tells the love interest that his feelings are real. That this stopped being pretend a long time ago."

"What makes *you* the main character and not me?" Qaed ventured to close the distance between them even more, his breath ghosting across Clement's soft lips.

"Fine. You can be the main character if it's that important to you, but that just means you have to be the one to confess first."

Now *that,* Qaed could do. "Clement... this may never have been pretend for me. Even that night at Cafe Strelka, I did most of what I did to make you smile, because I... have been *so* incredibly taken by it ever since the first time you smiled at me when you made us coffee on your first night here."

A sound escaped Clement that was half-laugh, half-sob. "That long?"

"That long." Qaed leaned his forehead against Clement's. "Can I kiss you? A *real* kiss, one meant for no one but you and I?"

"Please do," Clement said, and Qaed did as he was told.

Chapter Sixteen

Qaed

QAED DIDN'T INTEND TO have sex with Clement tonight. Gods, he could lose himself in the simple heat of Clement's mouth against his, of his warm hands on Qaed's body. He sat back against the cushions at the head of the bed and greedily pulled Clement into his arms. He would let himself revel in being allowed to hold Clement like this.

But it seemed Clement had something else in mind. He trailed languid kisses down the column of Qaed's throat, and Qaed bit back the urge to whimper. "I really have some reading to get back to," he tried, heat pooling in his lower belly.

"You can read later," Clement said, sliding his hands up Qaed's shirt and coaxing it off his body. "You have something more important to do right now."

Qaed's cocks stirred in response. "Yeah? What is that?" he asked, arching his back off the bed to aid in the removal of his shirt.

"Me." He grinned, and any determination Qaed had to be a gentleman and *not* fuck Clement tonight went flying out the window.

He couldn't help but laugh, slipping Clement's shirt off him as well. He never tired of seeing Clement shirtless; there was something undeniably sexy about the pink, slightly raised scars lining his chest, his almost perfectly round, pink nipples, the smattering of soft hair coating his chest. Clement reddened under the intensity of his stare, the color traveling to his chest.

"Well, when you say it like that, it is hard to argue," Qaed said, his cocks straining against his pants. Against Clement's thigh. It would take an army to pull Qaed away from Clement now.

Clement lowered himself to Qaed's level, planting a trail of kisses down the length of his torso. Qaed's breathing grew shallow as he continued his path down, his journey ending at the tent in Qaed's pants. He mouthed Qaed's erections and it took everything in him not to simply combust. "Shit, Clement," he gasped, resisting the urge to push himself into Clement's mouth.

That urge was only amplified by Clement tugging down the waistband of his pants, allowing Qaed's cocks to spring free. They leaked desperately, the throbbing almost too much to handle.

"I wanted to do this the first time," Clement whispered, taking the base of one of his cocks into his hand. His pretty pink mouth stretched around the head of it, his tongue swirling over the slit. Qaed groaned, carding his fingers through Clement's soft curls. His hand shifted to his neglected cock, and the sensation was simultaneously too much and not enough. He wanted to bury his cocks deep inside Clement, hear him screaming for more.

His orgasm built up embarrassingly quickly, and Qaed gave his hair a sharp tug. "Clement, you have to stop," he said, his voice thin. "I am–"

Clement moved his mouth away from Qaed, but his hand on his other cock didn't stop for a second. Qaed tipped his head back, fucking into Clement's fist like his life depended on it. "Come in my mouth, Qaed," he murmured, flattening his tongue against Qaed's shaft and giving it one long, slow lick.

Qaed wouldn't have lasted another second if he'd tried. Clement's movements on his cock didn't stop as he milked every last drop from Qaed, his pearlescent cum coating Clement's face and chest. He looked down at Clement just in time to see him open his mouth and prepare his tongue to catch it in his mouth.

Gods, if he was able to, that would have gotten him going all over again. "Fuck, Clement," he breathed. "I did not mean to be so quick, I–"

"I thought it was hot." Clement crawled off the bed and retrieved a towel from the bathroom, giving himself a quick wipe. "It made me feel like I did something right."

If Clement only knew. "You did everything right. Gods, I can hardly control myself around you," Qaed said, shifting to sit at the edge of the bed and allowing Clement to slot between his legs. He already missed the sight of Clement, painted with his cum.

Clement cradled Qaed's head in his hands and Qaed looked up, his eyes melting into Clement's.

He didn't know another creature could make him feel like this. A warmth blossomed in his chest that made him want to crawl out of his skin and into Clement's. No degree of closeness could ever feel quite close enough.

"Clement," he whispered. He didn't know what words were about to come out of his mouth. All he knew was that he needed to say *something*. "I... I cannot thank you enough for these last few months. They have meant the world to me. *You...* mean the world to me." He steeled his jaw against the wave of tears threatening at the base of his throat.

Clement smiled a watery smile down at him and kissed him gently. And it was nothing but that. A kiss. A kiss because he wanted to, not because he felt any obligation to. "You mean the world to me, too." He lowered his head to Qaed's, pressing their foreheads together. "We should throw Candy and Votra a thank you party."

Qaed laughed, wrapping his arms around Clement's waist. "We should. I feel like I owe them my life."

It was scary to think about where he might be if Clement hadn't come along. He liked to think he would have had enough self control to keep himself on the right path. But Clement was what made him want to be better. Clement made him want to *be* something.

He wanted to be the best version of himself for Clement, because that was what he deserved. Because he loved him.

Fuck, Qaed loved Clement. He loved him with an intensity that scared him. Clement had the power to break Qaed, and Gods, would he let him.

He unraveled himself from Clement's waist and moved further into the bed to allow Clement to join him. A hand skated along Clement's thigh, his pretty human's breath hitching at the contact. "Will you let me take care of you now?" Qaed asked. He was desperate to get out of his head again, and he was quickly learning that his favorite thing to get lost in was Clement.

Clement grinned that toothy grin at him, and Qaed could have sworn his insides were turning to goo. "If you insist," he said, falling back against the cushions and letting his legs fall open, allowing Qaed to move between them. He bit his lip. "You could... go down on me, if you want."

It took everything in Qaed to bite back his laughter. "If I *want*?" He lowered himself to Clement's level, his breath ghosting across the shell of Clement's ear. "Darling, I have been dying to put my mouth on you for weeks."

Despite the need raging through him, he took his time as he moved down Clement's body, taking the time to appreciate every inch. He kissed down his chest, his stomach, hooking his fingertips underneath the waistband of his pants and tugging them down. Clement helped to kick them off, and Qaed was all too ready to bury himself in him.

He moved carefully, slowly, pressing taunting kisses to Clement's inner thighs. He'd barely touched Clement and already, he was squirming under Qaed's touch. He shifted to the other thigh, nipping at the skin where it met the hem of his boxers. His mouth continued across the soaked fabric until it reached Clement's clothed heat.

"*Gods,* you are so ready for me," he breathed against Clement, his own cocks slowly coming to life again. He rested his nose against him, tongue pressing against his core.

"Holy shit," Clement cried out, hips snapping up against the ministrations of Qaed's tongue. "Fuck, Qaed, I need you on me. Please." Trembling fingers fumbled with the elastic of his boxers, and Qaed reveled in seeing him coming undone with such little action. He couldn't wait to see how Clement reacted when his mouth was on him properly.

He helped Clement slide his boxers down, revealing Clement's pretty, glistening cock, surrounded by a mass of wiry brown hair. "Look at you," he murmured, his thumb brushing over the head. Clement whined, thighs trembling with the effort of his own restraint. "I cannot wait to suck your pretty cock."

"Just fucking do it already," Clement groaned, and Qaed didn't try to suppress his laughter. He was so cute like this, so desperate for Qaed that his body couldn't contain all of his want.

He lowered his mouth onto Clement, taking him into his mouth in his entirety. He swiped his tongue across the head then traced slow, sloppy circles around it. Clement gripped Qaed's one long horn, giving it a sharp tug.

The motion went straight to Qaed's cocks. If they weren't so spent, they'd be hard as rocks by now. But he still couldn't keep himself from moaning, the vibration earning him a pleased noise from Clement.

Clement's thick thighs came up to clamp around Qaed's head, anchoring him in place. And that was exactly where Qaed wanted to be. He would happily never come up for air again. He clutched Clement's thighs with both hands, digging his fingertips into the soft flesh as he continued, his saliva mingling with the juices of Clement's arousal.

The slurping sounds filling the room were downright dirty, and Qaed loved every second of it. The only thing he loved more was the pitiful sounds streaming from Clement's pretty lips, the moans punctuated every now and then by a whimper of Qaed's name.

Those were his favorite parts.

He poked his tongue into Clement's entrance and Clement shoved himself into Qaed's mouth. "Fuck, right there," he gasped. "God damn, you're good with your mouth."

Qaed would have *loved* to take the time to gloat, but he was having too much fun wresting reactions like that from him. His tongue returned to Clement's throbbing erection, and Qaed introduced a finger inside Clement.

"Fuck!" Clement's hips stuttered at the intrusion, but he melted into it after a few seconds, his hips moving of their own accord against his finger. He was so tight, and he allowed himself the indulgence of being proud that the only cock, the only fingers that had been inside him were Qaed's.

And if he could, he'd do everything he could to keep it that way. This was *his* hole to fuck as he pleased, *his* pretty little cock.

His human.

Clement bared down on his finger, and Qaed took that as an invitation to introduce a second. It was received with a sharp cry of surprise that soon melted into yet another stream of cute little moans. A hand came down to clutch his, blunt fingernails digging into the flesh of his hand.

"Qaed, I'm so close," he gasped, his grip on Qaed tightening.

Qaed didn't pull away from Clement for a second. He didn't want this to be over, but more than that, he wanted this to be an orgasm Clement would never forget.

He curled his fingers inside Clement, the tips of his fingers brushing the spot he knew would drive Clement wild.

The world muffled around him as the grip of Clement's thighs around his head tightened. He could barely make out Clement's wanton moans of 'there, right there' just before he came, his arousal gushing into Qaed's mouth.

Qaed lapped him up like his life depended on it, withdrawing his fingers slowly from his pulsating hole and allowing him to ride out the aftershocks of his orgasm on Qaed's face. His hold on Qaed's hand loosened, the other hand on Qaed's horn dropping completely.

He only removed himself when Clement's trembling thighs fell from around his head, his body entirely spent. "Holy shit." Clement's voice was raw, and Qaed couldn't help but think he could get used to hearing him like that.

"What was that you were saying a little while ago?" Qaed asked, moving to sit at Clement's side. "That I am good with my mouth?"

"No, actually, you're terrible with your mouth. Do I need to teach you how to give head, because I had a *horrible* time." Clement grinned. "Come here and kiss me. My bones are jelly now, thanks to you."

Qaed was all too happy to oblige. "I would not think that bad head would make your bones into jelly," he murmured against Clement's lips.

"Shut up." Clement kissed him, and he could taste both himself and Clement on his lips.

Chapter Seventeen

Clement

CLEMENT AWOKE ENTANGLED IN Qaed's arms, and for a split second, he wondered if he really needed to go to this event in the first place.

He rolled over to face Qaed, as if the butterflies in his stomach from staring at him would override the anxiety bubbling in him. And to an extent, it worked. But he also kind of felt like his stomach acid was dissolving the butterflies.

Qaed's grip on him tightened, tucking Clement even closer to his chest. "Good morning," he muttered into Clement's hair.

"'Morning." He pressed a kiss to the underside of Qaed's jaw. "What if I just stayed here all day?"

"No. You are getting up." As if to make a point, Qaed unraveled his arms from around him, and Clement whined at the loss of contact. His mouth stretched into a yawn and he rubbed his eyes. God, how was Clement supposed to leave when he had the most beautiful man in the world still naked in his bed?

Clement begrudgingly sat up, trailing a hand down the length of Qaed's torso. Now that he'd had a taste of what sleeping with Qaed was like, he was like a man possessed. All he wanted was to be under Qaed again, tasting himself on Qaed's lips.

He had to stop before he got riled up all over again. "Whatever you are thinking, stop it," Qaed said, the corner of his lips quirked into a sleepy smile. "We have time later. For when I get to reward you for doing this."

Damn him. Clement leaned down and kissed him before shoving himself out of bed. "Fine. It better be a hell of a reward." But knowing Qaed, it would be.

He dressed in the one button-up he owned and a pair of slacks and dragged a brush through his hair, which was even more disheveled this morning than normal. He spritzed himself with cologne and brushed his teeth. Hopefully, he didn't look as nervous as he felt. He clenched and unclenched his hands at his sides, staring at his reflection in the mirror.

What if they didn't like him? What if not a single agent was interested in picking up his book? He exhaled slowly, shakily, and a pair of muscular arms found their way around him. Qaed was still shirtless, but he'd slipped his pajama pants back on. Thank God, because if Qaed had pressed those two dicks against him from behind, he wouldn't be going *anywhere*.

"You smell good," Qaed murmured, pressing the bridge of his nose against Clement's shoulder. "They are going to love you."

Somehow, even Qaed saying it didn't entirely reassure him. "I hope you're right," he said. He turned in Qaed's arms, resting his hands on either side of his face. "I gotta go."

"Good luck." Qaed kissed him, and Clement all but melted into him.

Clement drummed his hands on Qaed's strong chest. "Alright, go lay back down before I change my mind." Qaed released him with a chuckle and Clement tugged on his pair of nice dress shoes before heading into the hallway.

He immediately wished Qaed was there with him. But he had to do this alone, if only to prove to himself that he could. He'd been ready for this before, he reminded himself. He'd written pitch after pitch for other books, and he'd pored over the pitch for this one for weeks. He could recite it in his sleep.

When Clement reached the lobby, the conference was in full swing. He checked in at the desk and was given a name tag with pronouns, as well as a brochure of events. Maybe he'd go to some other panels, but right now, the pitch event was the only thing on his mind.

And apparently, he wasn't the only person. The only signs in the lobby pointed towards the ballroom, where the pitch event would take place. Clement drew in as deep of a breath as his lungs would hold and followed the signs.

They led to a wide, brightly lit hallway, where other convention attendees lined each side of the wall. Immediately, a familiar figure waved him down. "Clement!" Zanna called from about halfway down the hallway. Her indigo curls were pulled into a tidy bun, her two antennae poking out from the top of her head. She was much more sharply dressed than Clement was used to seeing her, in a blue blazer and skirt set that matched her hair.

The sight of someone he knew served to settle his nerves, if only a little. "Thank God you're here," he said as he approached her, and she was quick to pull him in for a hug. "Do you *also* feel like you're gonna throw up?"

"Yep. Didn't dare to eat any breakfast, just in case." She smoothed her hands over her blouse, and Clement could see the tremble in them as she did. "Fuck. Holy shit, this is happening. *Hooooooly shit.*"

Clement grinned, squeezing her shoulders. "It's okay. We can do this," he said, not entirely sure he believed the words himself. But they were easier to say when he was trying to encourage someone else. "And if one of us gets an agent and the other one doesn't, we'll never speak of this again."

"Deal."

The event organizer, a drask with scales as golden as the walls, interrupted, his booming voice cutting through the low hum of chatter in the hallway. "Thank you all for attending Yakut Writer's Conference's pitch event! We know you have all been preparing for a long time and are excited to get started, so I won't waste much of your time. The agents are waiting at booths, and you will file in and take your positions at the chair in front of them. You will have five minutes to pitch your manuscript and ask any questions you have, and then you will move on to the next booth. We have allotted enough time to allow everyone to speak to all of the agents, but you are free to go once you have spoken to everyone you wish to."

Now Clement was *really* going to throw up. He forced a breath through his mouth, and Zanna reached for his clammy hand and squeezed it. He wasn't going to let her go until he absolutely had to.

"We will be opening the doors in sixty seconds. Best of luck to you all."

The sixty seconds that followed were simultaneously the longest and shortest sixty seconds of his life, and he was pretty sure he'd already sweated through his shirt. He tugged on his blazer despite the heat burning through him and followed the crowd into the ballroom on shaky legs.

There were probably twenty agents in the ballroom, all of whom Clement had done extensive research on. Only about half of them were looking for the kind of book Clement wrote, and a couple of them weren't looking to sign new authors. His odds weren't fantastic, but if he could just get through this... then he could celebrate the fact that he'd done it in the first place.

That was what he told himself over and over as he found himself in front of his first agent. A human woman, the first human he'd seen in months, with a slicked-back black bun and piercing green eyes that felt very much like they were peering into Clement's very soul. "Hi," Clement said, his voice small. "Would you like to hear my pitch?"

"I would," she said, lacing her manicured fingers together and leaning forward. "Go ahead, whenever you're ready."

So he did. He launched into his pitch like he had all the times he'd recited it to Qaed, to Candy, to Zanna–it was a good pitch, he knew. He only stumbled over his words once, when the agent tapped something into the datapad she was holding. Maybe she was marking him off her list, deciding halfway through the pitch that it was actually terrible.

He cleared his throat upon finishing, and her eyes curved into crescents as she smiled at him. "Strong pitch," she said. "You certainly have something here. But I may not be the most perfect person to represent you."

Okay. That wasn't horrible feedback. "Okay. Thank you for your time anyway."

"Of course. I promise, with your enthusiasm, you'll hook someone." And God, did he hope she was right.

The rest of his pitches, though, weren't quite so smooth. The next agent stopped him mid-pitch, telling him that retellings were overdone. The third let him get his entire pitch out, only to tell him that he didn't feel that he could sell the book.

When the fourth told him his book simply wasn't for them but could be for someone else, Clement wanted to disappear into the floor. The rejections sat in his stomach like lead, and he wasn't sure he could handle another one. His gaze flicked to the door and, once his time with the fourth agent ended, he bolted.

One in four were good odds, he tried to tell himself as he leaned against the wall of the hallway outside the ballroom. "God dammit," he muttered, bending at the waist and placing his hands on his knees.

The other writers wouldn't let a few rejections get in their way. Everyone else was powering through. So why couldn't he?

His legs carried him back to the hotel room instead of back into the ballroom like they should have. The tension settling across his chest lifted with every floor he went up in the elevator. He couldn't go back down there. He couldn't face any more of those agents. He couldn't face Zanna.

He couldn't face Qaed, either. He stopped short of the door, his throat tight. How could he go in there and tell Qaed he'd dragged him across the planet, only to run away not even half an hour in?

Rather than going back into the room, Clement continued down the hallway past their door. The mouth of the hallway opened up to an outdoor seating area, one that was mercifully empty thanks to the fact that most of the hotel's patrons were probably in the lobby. The seating area was a welcome reprieve to the blinding gold of the rest of the hotel; the floors were wooden instead, dotted with loungers not unlike the ones you'd find by an Earth pool.

Clement sat back in one of the loungers and freed himself from the confines of his blazer. He held it in his lap and stared at it, the blazer blurring as his tears splattered onto the fabric.

This was stupid. He should've kept going. And now, he had even *less* of a chance because he'd only talked to a quarter of the agents in the room. He'd wasted so much time, so much energy... so much of *Qaed's* time.

As if on queue, Clement's comm vibrated with a message from Qaed. He almost couldn't bring himself to read it. But the part of him that couldn't stand the thought of being seen by Qaed wanted him there, wanted to be comforted by him.

QAED: Thinking about you.

QAED: If any of these agents give you a hard time, give me their names. I am not above roughing them up. :muscle arm emoji:

QAED: Joking. Mostly.

Clement laughed through his tears and sent a message back.

CLEMENT: I'm already done.

QAED: Wait, really? That was fast.

QAED: Are you alright? Where are you?

CLEMENT: Seating area on the 12th floor

He erupted into tears once again and kind of hated himself for it. What was Qaed going to think of him after all this?

The door leading out to the seating area slid open only a couple minutes later. "Clem," Qaed said softly, crouching on the ground beside the lounger. "What happened?"

"I gave up," Clement managed weakly. "I don't know what I was expecting. It's not like the agents were going to fall over themselves to get to me. I was bound to get rejections. I guess I just... wasn't prepared to hear them out loud." He sniffled, wiping his eyes with the heels of his palms. "I left after talking to four agents."

"That is four more than you started with," Qaed pointed out. "You should still be proud of yourself."

He couldn't bring himself to be. Clement huffed, laying back against the scratchy fabric of the lounger. "This just feels like a waste. All of it. I dragged you all the way out here for me to give up less than halfway through."

"Stop that." Qaed forced his way onto the bottom half of the lounger, pushing Clement's legs aside to perch precariously on the edge of it. "You *wrote* something, did you not? After all these years of not writing anything, you wrote an entire book in four months."

"Yeah, a book that I was only able to write because I forced you to go on a bunch of stupid, fake dates with me," Clement shot back. More than anything, he was embarrassed. He didn't know what he'd expected–maybe that his book would sell for hundreds of thousands of credits, and he'd finally be able to repay Qaed for everything he'd done for him. "I'm just a giant phony, and I dragged you into it."

Qaed's face turned unreadable. "It was not all false," he said, his voice strained.

"It was, though!" Clement threw his hands into the air. "God, I asked you to have *sex* with me because I couldn't write it on my own."

"I wanted to." Qaed's jaw visibly clenched. "That was not fake for me."

And that only made things worse. Qaed didn't deserve to have his feelings preyed upon, to be used by Clement for a book he didn't even have the confidence to sell. "I'm sorry I did that to you," he managed through trembling lips.

Qaed rose from the lounger. "I understand now," he said. "You could not even tell me that last night was real for you. You made *me* say it." He blinked more rapidly than normal, shifting his gaze skyward. "This is my fault. Every time we get even remotely close to each other, you are *so* quick to say, 'this is just for research.' And I should have listened to you."

Clement's blood turned to ice. He sat up, his heart drumming in his ears. This wasn't how this was supposed to go. "Wait, that's not–"

"Not what? Not what you meant? What *did* you mean, then?"

The thing was, that *was* what he meant. None of this was supposed to be real. He had been so willing to drag Qaed along on this journey without doing any of the actual work himself. He'd been so determined that Qaed deserved better than this, better than for Clement to *actually* fall in love with him, that he'd held him at a verbal arms' length.

"I meant that I wasted your time!" Clement stood as well, placing a few feet of distance between him and Qaed. "These past four months, you've been so... *perfect.* You've cooked for me, you've taken me out, you've listened to me talk about things I've never told anyone about. And that was all for nothing because I walked out of the pitch event. I wasted four months of your life for *nothing.*"

"Clement, what do I have to do to get through your skull that I *wanted* to do all of these things for you? These last four months were not a waste for me. If they were nothing but novel fodder for you, fine. I can live with that. But do not project that onto me. When I told you last night that this was always real for me, I meant it."

Shit. "Qaed–"

The door to the seating area closed behind Qaed with a slam.

Chapter Eighteen

Qaed

Gods, Qaed wanted a drink. He hadn't had a craving this aggressive in months, and he refused to give into it. Not over this. Not over Clement.

He found himself at the rooftop bar, exercising self restraint just to remind himself that he could. He ordered a carbonated water and took up a small, two-seater table facing out towards the setting sun. Towards the same sky he'd kissed Clement under only the night before.

He didn't want to be here. The bar was populated with couples and people in suits–conference attendees. Both things reminded him too much of Clement. But he couldn't go back to the hotel room and he *definitely* couldn't go back to the seating area Clement was in.

He should have known better. Why would someone like Clement truly, genuinely want to spend that much time around him? It wasn't as if he'd tried to dance around the truth. Every outing that felt like a date, every night spent watching a movie on the couch, every breakfast Qaed cooked with Clement sitting on the counter next to him was punctuated by the reminder that Clement just wanted the experience. Qaed was just collateral damage.

He sipped his water and watched the sun as it began to dip beneath the horizon. Clement would have loved to see this, he thought. And then he snorted, selfishly glad that Clement was missing it. But he couldn't stop a small, nagging part of him from wishing Clement was there.

Qaed rubbed a hand over his face. The conference would end tomorrow, and then they'd have a painfully awkward ride home and they could return to being roommates. Just roommates. Nothing more.

He wasn't confident that he'd be able to do that. He'd get one look at Clement, standing at the kitchen counter, making his coffee in the morning and he'd be overcome with the urge to slide his arms around him, rest his chin on his shoulder. Kiss that little spot at the base of his ear that made him shiver.

"Gods dammit, Clement," he muttered under his breath, rubbing his eyes until he saw stars. It had been so long since he'd sat in his feelings like this, and he remembered why he hated it so much. His chest ached, his eyes burned, his stomach felt like he'd swallowed a pile of rocks.

"You called?" Clement attempted a little smile as he materialized beside Qaed. He hovered awkwardly beside the chair opposite Qaed.

Qaed couldn't tell if he was happy to see him or not. "More like I was cursing your existence," he said, burying his expression in his drink.

"Yeah, okay. That's fair." Clement rested a hand on the back of the other chair. "I wanted to talk to you... about all that. But if you want to be alone, I understand that, too."

Qaed trailed a finger through the condensation gathering on his glass. "You can stay," he said, feigning nonchalance the best that he could. "At least sit down. You are making me nervous."

Clement did as he was told, climbing into the tall chair next to Qaed. "Sorry." He laced his fingers together in front of him, fidgeting as he spoke. "I was an asshole. And I completely understand why you're pissed."

Something told Qaed he didn't. He stayed quiet, taking another thoughtful sip of his drink.

"I completely wrote you off back there." He stared down at his hands. "I was so caught up in my own failure... I wanted to show you that I appreciated everything you've done for me, but I ended up circling around to being a dick."

"Yeah, you did." Qaed ducked his head, not wanting to let Clement see him cry *again*. "What made you think I did not mean any of the things I did for you?"

"Nothing. God, nothing at all. I had myself convinced that you were *so* dedicated to helping me that you were just... a really good actor. I didn't think that someone like you could want... *me*."

"I spelled it out for you quite clearly," Qaed said. "I told you last night that I wanted you, that I'd wanted you since the beginning."

"I didn't know how to let myself believe it." Clement's voice was small now, barely audible over the constant din of the bar guests around them. "It was so easy to convince myself that you were just *really* dedicated to the bit. Because you're so... good. God, you're too fucking good for me and you *have* to know that."

Qaed swallowed thickly. "You should believe people when they tell you things. Not everyone is lying to you."

"I know." Clement lifted his head, his tired eyes meeting Qaed's. "I'm sorry for not trusting you."

Qaed longed to reach across the table and brush the tears from his cheeks. But he didn't. He folded his hands in his lap as if to restrain himself. "Do you trust me *now*?" he asked, bracing himself for the answer.

"I do." Clement's answer was quick, firm. "I would literally put my life in your hands, which is kinda terrifying."

"It is. You absolutely should not put your life in my hands." Qaed smiled despite himself.

Clement laughed softly, and it was only then that Qaed realized how much he'd missed hearing it. "Okay, okay, I'll try to avoid it if I can." He slid out of his chair and rounded the table to Qaed's side. "Will you come back to the room with me? I need to tell you something but I don't wanna do it out here."

Qaed raised his brow at Clement. "Why not here?"

"Because," Clement said, taking one of Qaed's hands in his own. "You deserve for this to be different."

Qaed wasn't entirely sure what Clement was talking about, but he stood from his chair anyway. "Alright. This had better be worth it."

He followed Clement back down the elevator to their room, and Qaed braced himself against the door, as if he might need to escape. He folded his arms over his chest, his back against the wood, and stared at Clement, daring him to speak.

And he did. "I know I'm not good at this. I know you're pissed at me, and I understand. You have every right to be. But I wanna prove to you how real this was for me, too." He pulled his laptop out of his bag and Qaed suppressed the urge to roll his eyes. He wasn't sure he wanted to hear another word about this damn book.

Clement held his laptop in one arm, scrolling through his manuscript with the other hand. "Okay, okay. Chapter Twelve." He cleared his throat. "Dholzi crouched over their barely-flickering fire, stirring something in a heavy-bottomed pot. Vandu stared openly at the muscles rippling across his broad back, the way it tapered into narrow hips that she wanted to rest her hands on. 'Can I help you?' Dholzi asked, and she could practically hear the smirk playing at his lips.

"'Don't you know it's stupid to cook without a shirt on?' she asked in lieu of blurting out just how gorgeous his back was from where she stood."

Qaed tried to suppress the smile creeping onto his lips and failed. Clement cleared his throat and continued.

"'These are flesh-eating spiders,' Dholzi said, idly poking the dry dirt beneath their boots with a stick. 'I knew a guy once who ate one on a dare. They found him the next day and the spider had eaten right through him.'

"Vandu blanched, feeling vaguely ill. 'We should move our camp, then,' she said, trying to ignore the phantom sensation of tiny, spindly legs crawling up and down her limbs.

"Dholzi grinned. 'You really think there are flesh-eating spiders out here?' He picked one up and let it rest on the flat of his palm. 'It's so easy to fuck with you.'

"I didn't use any of the stuff we did for the book. Not that night at the fair, not the fake proposal at Cafe Strelka. All of the parts about being with you that inspired me were... just you being you. I was able to write about Vandu falling in love with Dholzi because I knew what it felt like. Because I was falling in love with *you*." Clement put his laptop down, taking a step towards Qaed. "It was always real for me, too. I just didn't know it."

Qaed couldn't stop himself from stealing Clement into his arms, dragging him in for a searing kiss. Clement sobbed against his lips and Qaed kissed his tears away. "Gods, took you long enough to figure it out," he whispered against the salty skin of his cheek.

"Shut up," Clement laughed, draping his arms around Qaed's neck. "You gonna say it back?"

"I thought I might make you squirm for a minute," Qaed said. He pressed a kiss behind Clement's ear, and he shivered violently in Qaed's arms.

"I was just kidding, by the way. There's no rush to–"

"I love you, too."

"You interrupt a lot." Clement pulled back, resting his hands against the flat of Qaed's chest. "Sorry, I didn't quite hear what you said–"

"Now you are pushing it." Qaed pulled away from Clement, capturing his chin between his thumb and finger.

"Your family is lovely," Dholzi murmured, letting his lips brush across Vandu's forehead. "But Straal's nowhere near as hot as you. I'm kinda glad you took his place."

Vandu laughed, resting her hands against Dholzi's bare chest. "You're glad I fought in the war instead of him? That's kind of fucked up, don't you think?"

"Alright, alright. I wish I would have gotten to fight alongside him, gain his trust, and persuade him to let me come home with him after the war, so I could meet his gorgeous sister and make her fall in love with me." The bridge of Dholzi's nose rested against Vandu's forehead. "But I'm grateful. For you, for the time we spent in the barracks, on the surface of Vegneid. As much as I loved fighting by your side, I'm looking forward to a life where we never have to fight again."

Vandu trailed her fingertips along Dholzi's strong back. "We won't. We're done fighting. I promise."

–Excerpt from *To Spite a Raven's Heart* by Clement Hall

Chapter Nineteen

Clement

CLEMENT WASN'T ENTIRELY SURE how many hours of sleep he'd gotten last night, but he wasn't sure a single one of them was solid. Not that he was complaining, of course. Having a gorgeous, two-dicked man in his bed who couldn't keep his hands off him was the opposite of a problem.

Until his sleep deprived reflection stared back at him in the mirror as he brushed his teeth. The bags under his eyes and puffy eyelids made him look like a zombie. At least he wasn't going anywhere today.

He trudged back into the living area and flopped onto the bed next to Qaed. For all he cared, he could spend the rest of the day in bed, doing exactly what he'd done all night last night. He climbed atop Qaed's half-asleep form, and a pair of chilly arms came up to wrap around him.

"Good morning," Qaed said in his sleepy gravel. Clement was surely never going to grow tired of that.

"'Morning." Clement pressed a kiss to the underside of Qaed's jaw.

Qaed's lips curved into a slow smile. "Are you going to get ready?" he asked, sliding his hands up the back of Clement's shirt.

Clement shivered at the introduction of Qaed's cold fingers. "Get ready? For what? A repeat of last night?"

Qaed chuckled, his eyes finally opening. "What, the... six orgasms last night did not satisfy you?"

"It was seven."

"So you are even greedier than I thought." In one swift movement, Qaed turned Clement onto his back, hovering over him in nothing but the boxer briefs that barely contained his two powerful cocks. Oh, Clement certainly wasn't going *anywhere* this morning.

"If being greedy is a crime, throw me in the slammer." Clement leaned up, draping his arms around Qaed's neck. One of Qaed's large hands came up to support him, resting between his shoulderblades. His mouth hovered centimeters over Clement's and stopped just short of kissing him.

"If you want an eighth, you will go back down to the convention today." He kissed the corner of Clement's mouth and Clement groaned, letting himself fall back against the pillows.

"Just say you hate me. It'd hurt less," he whined, and Qaed laughed, pushing a stray curl out of Clement's eyes.

"I say this out of love, beloved," Qaed said, standing up from the bed and crossing the room to his suitcase. He bent down, giving Clement a guilt-free view of his juicy, muscular ass. "The pitch event is going on today as well, yes?"

"Well, yeah, but that doesn't mean I wanna go to it." Clement wrapped the comforter around himself as if to protect himself from the thought. The last thing he wanted to do was face the agents he'd run away from yesterday. He'd already embarrassed himself. He didn't need another opportunity to do so.

Qaed tugged the sleeveless black high-necked top from his bag that he *knew* Clement loved on him. It showed off those muscular arms Clement loved to hold onto. This man was *actually* evil. "You only spoke to a handful of agents yesterday. You can speak to the rest of them today." He tugged the top on and shoved his legs into a pair of baggy black pants. "You *should*."

Clement knew that he should. A small part of him wanted to, but a much larger, much more demanding part of him wanted to hide and never put another word to paper again. He tucked the comforter under his chin. "What if they remember me from yesterday as the guy who ran out before the half way point?"

"Then perhaps they will be impressed that you came back." Qaed took Clement's button-down and pants from the chair he'd slung them over yesterday and held them out to him. "Clement, this book deserves to be seen by the world. Give it a chance."

Clement scoffed, trying his best to ignore the heat rising to his cheeks. "Does it really?" He eyed the clothes offered to him for a moment before taking them.

"At the very least, they deserve to know Dholzi. He was my favorite character, by far." Qaed grinned and Clement swatted him with his shirt before pulling it on. "I am not trying to pressure you into anything. But I think you would regret it if you left without trying again."

Clement hated that Qaed was right. The regret wouldn't hit him until a few weeks later, when he was deep in the trenches of searching for representation because he'd given this opportunity up. He crawled out of bed and pulled his pants on. "Just so you know, you're not allowed to say 'I told you so' if anything good happens," he said, combing his fingers through his hair.

"I would not dream of it," Qaed said, shooting Clement a cheeky smile that very much told him he planned on doing exactly that. He kissed Clement properly this time. "I am kicking you out of this hotel room and you are not allowed to come back for at least two hours. Understood?"

"Fine." Clement jutted his lower lip out in a pout and Qaed took the opportunity to tug on his lip. "Annoying ass."

"I love you," Qaed said, and Clement's heart clenched. Maybe that would be the good luck he needed.

"I love you, too." Clement brushed his teeth, spritzed himself with cologne, and forced himself out of the room before he could talk himself out of it again. Qaed was right. He *should* try again. Even if it was just a try.

He forced as deep of a breath as he could manage into his lungs as he descended the elevator to the lobby. Anxiety crept into the pit of his chest, but he breathed through it. "You can do this, Clement," he murmured, letting out one final exhale once the doors parted.

Maybe it was just wishful thinking, but the convention felt less crowded this time. The line for the pitch event was shorter, and there weren't quite so many clusters of attendees. He retrieved a nametag from the registration desk again and walked toward the ballroom.

Clement pressed himself against the wall next to the other attendees, running over his pitch again in his head. Maybe a hefty dose of delusion would get him through this. It was a good pitch. A great one, even. And the agents who had turned him down yesterday didn't know what they were talking about. In fact, they should be begging him–

"Clement!" Zanna's voice interrupted his spiral. "I was worried about you yesterday! Where'd you go?"

He grimaced. It was hard to face her knowing she'd been the one to invite him and all he'd done was let her down. His shoulders tensed as he turned to her. Her dark curls were loose around her thin face today, this time wearing a red blouse and black pencil skirt. He was surprised that she even needed to pitch again–surely someone had snatched her up yesterday.

"I, uh... got a little overwhelmed," he said. "But I'm trying again today."

"Good, you should. Your book is amazing." Zanna gave his hand a reassuring squeeze. "I believe in you."

And maybe Clement could, too. He steeled himself as the attendees started to file into the ballroom, his desire to run activating as he came face to face with the same sets of tables and chairs as he had yesterday. The same chairs he'd sat in and been told his story was uninteresting, unoriginal, or otherwise unmarketable.

But today would be different, he told himself. Today would be the day that someone appreciated him and the art he created. He took a seat in the first chair, opposite a tall, pink-skinned aquatic alien who didn't appear terribly excited to be there.

And if they weren't, it was fine. There were twelve other agents for Clement to talk to, and dammit, he was going to talk to every single one of them. He launched into his pitch, inwardly wincing at how tight his voice was. His nerves were shot, and all he wanted to do was run away again.

But he forced himself through, even when the agent clicked their tongue at him. "Thank you for your time, but I don't believe I'm the best fit for you. Best of luck, though." Their three unblinking eyes flicked to something behind Clement, silently dismissing him.

It was fine. He could make it through a rejection. Or two. The second agent was polite enough to act mildly interested but passed on him as well. He took in a breath, his fingertips tingling with nerves. Maybe Qaed *wouldn't* dump him if he ran away now. He'd *just* said 'I love you' for the first time. Surely, that would damper his disappointment just a little bit.

But he forced himself into the next seat, across from an elegant, purple-skinned qintaril with a sharp face but kind eyes. He knew this woman. This was Alitaya Strix's agent. He'd done his research on every agent at the event, but Kora had been the main subject of his research.

This pitch could make or break his career. *No pressure,* he reminded himself, though he was *very much* feeling the pressure.

"Good morning," Kora said, lacing her fingers and resting her chin on top of them. "You may proceed whenever you are ready."

You can do this, Clement. "Thank you." He cleared his throat, forcing himself to maintain eye contact with her as he rattled off his pitch. Maybe he was just imagining things, but her eyes seemed to widen the more he spoke. Her attention on him didn't waver for a second, and Clement managed to convince himself it was because she was so entranced by him, by his story.

Or maybe she was going through her mental rolodex of rejections to decide which one suited Clement more. She didn't speak up until he took a final, quivering breath. "Twelfth Night, right?" she asked.

Clement blinked. "Yeah. You know Shakespeare?"

"I do. I have a bit of a soft spot for retellings, especially Shakespearean ones. I spent a lot of time studying Earth literature in university," she said, a smile pulling at her lips. "You have my interest. I would love to see the entire manuscript."

Holy shit. Clement's heart rushed in his ears so aggressively, he could hardly hear himself as he mustered up the courage to respond. "Of course! I'll send it over immediately," he said, numbly tapping his comm to hers as they exchanged information. Her face, along with her name–Kora–flashed on his screen.

"Fantastic. I will be on Veterok-III for a few days, as I have some work things to tie up, so I hope to read it over those days."

"Thank you so much," Clement said, the sentence tumbling out of him in a rush of breath he didn't notice he'd been holding.

He didn't let himself cry until he stood up and moved away from Kora, and even then, he only allowed a tear or two to roll down his cheeks before he collected himself. All he wanted to do was leave and tell Qaed.

But he had to finish what he started. He couldn't let himself leave yet. He made his way through the rest of his pitches, receiving only one more manuscript request between the ten agents remaining. The other agent that showed interest in him was a human woman from New Zealand who had a particular soft spot for romances between aliens and humans. "I met my wife out here on Veterok-III," she'd told him with a sparkle in her dark brown eyes. "She'd probably love this story, too."

After that particular conversation, all he wanted to do was see Qaed. Once the meetings were all done, he rushed out of the ballroom as quickly as his legs would carry him. Hell, he'd run up all thirteen flights of stairs if it would get him to his room faster.

But he didn't have to. He was moving so fast, he nearly missed Qaed, tucked into the corner of one of the elegant, red velvet chaise longues in the lobby, Clement's laptop in his lap. Whatever he was doing on it had him fully enraptured, his thumb pressed against the corner of his mouth.

Clement grinned, plopping onto the couch next to him. "We're already at the 'what's yours is mine' phase of our relationship, huh?" he teased, and Qaed blinked at Clement, rubbing at one of his eyes.

"I wanted to finish reading and this was the only way I knew how." He closed Clement's laptop and tucked it under his arm before standing, holding a hand out to Clement. "How did it go?"

The second Clement's hand found Qaed's, he burst into tears. Qaed set Clement's laptop down and pulled him into his arms carefully, resting a hand on the back of his head. He didn't seem to know how to react, which was the only thing that drew Clement from his tears. He laughed a particularly wet laugh. "I got two full manuscript requests," he said, grinning up at Qaed.

"Thank the gods. I did not prepare a consoling speech, but I certainly did prepare a congratulatory one," Qaed said, placing his hands on either side of Clement's cheeks. He brushed the tears from them with the pads of his thumbs.

"You can give that speech whenever you feel like it," Clement said, one of his hands encircling Qaed's.

Qaed leaned in, his forehead coming to rest against Clement's. "I am so proud of you," he whispered. "And I love you. And... I told you so."

"Asshole."

Chapter Twenty

Clement

AFTER THEIR TUMULTUOUS WEEKEND, Clement was more than ready to go home. He wanted to get back into his own bed–or Qaed's.

He dressed in a pair of comfortable sweatpants and a loose-fitting t-shirt for the ride home, and it seemed that Qaed had the same idea. There he was, in those damn gray sweatpants again. "Did I ever mention to you that these pants are part of what made me fall in love with you?" Clement asked with a coy smile, walking his fingers up Qaed's stomach to rest on his chest. "You look really hot in them."

"Can I tell you a secret?" Qaed leaned in, his mouth brushing the shell of Clement's ear. "I used to wear these around you a lot because you really are not subtle. I caught you staring a few times."

Clement gasped, a hand to his chest in feigned shock. "Pervert. You wanted me to stare at you?"

"Yes. I liked the attention." He kissed Clement's neck before pulling away from him, instead focusing his energy on gathering all of their bags into his strong arms. "Are you ready to go?"

"Yep, I think so." He tilted his chin towards the bags in Qaed's arms. "You want me to grab any of those?"

"I have them, love," Qaed said, and Clement's stomach flopped. He was never going to get tired of that.

Clement went to the front desk to check them out while Qaed took their things out to his shuttle. He was just passing over his keycard when a hand found his shoulder. "Clement! I was worried I wasn't gonna catch you before you left!"

He turned, coming face to face with Zanna. Kora was standing next to her, standing a full foot taller than Zanna in tall, professional heels. "Zanna, hey," Clement said, attention flicking to Kora. "Are you heading out, too?"

"Not 'til tomorrow. But... Kora was looking for you, so I figured I would help her find you. We... got to know each other yesterday, and when I brought you up, she mentioned your book, so...." She looked expectantly up at Kora.

Clement's body turned to ice, and he immediately regretted the fact that he was in ratty sweats and a t-shirt he'd stolen from Cecily in high school. "Hi! Sorry, I'm not, uh, dressed for meeting with you again," he laughed, clasping his already clammy hands together. "It's nice to see you again."

"Likewise. Zanna and I spent much of last night talking about *To Spite a Raven's Heart* because I simply could not put it down," Kora said, and Clement didn't know whether to be more shocked by the fact that Kora had already read the book or the fact that *something* had definitely happened between her and Zanna. He sent a questioning stare in her direction, but she pretended like she didn't see it.

"Wow, you read it already?" he asked. "Gosh, that's... really awesome. Thank you for reading it."

"No, thank *you* for allowing me to. I intended only to read the first chapter or two, but I simply could not stop, so please pardon how exhausted I might look this morning," Kora said. Zanna's cheeks went a darker shade of blue. *Damn. Good for her.* "I wanted to offer you representation before you left today. I feel confident that I can sell this book."

Clement's heart was *definitely* going to fall out of his ass. "No way," were the first words out of his mouth, and he immediately regretted them. "I mean, yeah, of course! I would love to be represented by you!"

"Wonderful. I will send some terms via comm. I do not wish to hold you up." Kora's attention shifted to something behind Clement, and it was only then that he became aware of Qaed's returned presence. He kept his distance, lingering by the front door. "It was lovely to meet you, Clement. Expect to hear from me again today."

Clement turned to watch her as she rejoined Zanna and they headed back into the hotel. Qaed looked at him, eyes widening a fraction in a questioning look. Clement answered him with a brilliant grin.

"One of the agents yesterday officially offered me representation," he said in a loud whisper. She was out of earshot now, but he still didn't want to risk embarrassing himself. "She's gonna send official terms over to me today."

"Clement! That is incredible!" Qaed snatched Clement into his arms so suddenly, he yelped in surprise. He spun Clement in a circle and planted a firm kiss on his lips. "Once we get home... we should celebrate, hm?"

Clement grinned. He could think of a few ways he'd like to celebrate.

By the time they arrived home, Clement was more than ready to crawl into bed. His eyes burned from the sheer amount of time he'd spent staring at his comm, waiting for Kora to confirm that she'd read his book. No matter how many times Qaed tried to pull his attention from it, he couldn't relax.

But being back in his own apartment with no one but Qaed brought him a peace that almost put him to sleep the moment they stepped in the door. "Thank God," he groaned, resisting the urge to lay down on the cold steel floor beneath him.

Qaed dropped their luggage to the floor with an unceremonious thump. "I will take that to the bedroom later," he said, pulling Clement into his embrace. "There is only one thing I am interested in taking to the bedroom right now."

"Yeah?" Clement smirked, resting his hands at either side of Qaed's neck. "You better be talking about me."

"You know I am." Qaed hooked his hands under Clement's thighs and lifted him, Clement's legs instinctively wrapping around Qaed's waist. God, how lucky was he that he'd managed to land a boyfriend that could carry him? "You are not too tired, are you?"

"No, sir," Clement said, peppering kisses along the column of Qaed's neck. Qaed groaned, the vibration of it delicious against Clement's lips. "Oh, you like that? Me calling you *sir*?"

"If you do not want me to fuck you on this floor, you will stop calling me *sir* until we get back to the bedroom," Qaed said, and Clement nipped at the base of his throat in response.

"Yes, *sir*." Clement could handle a little floor sex.

But Qaed took him back to his room anyway, laying him on the bed and imme-diately crawling across him. "What can I do to get you to *keep* calling me that?" he asked. Fuck, Qaed looked so good on top of him, the outline of his half-hard cocks clearly visible through his sweatpants. When Clement died, he wanted the rest of his money to go to whoever invented gray sweatpants.

Clement tented one leg, his knee brushing against those needy cocks. "I dunno. What are you gonna do for me?" he asked coyly, raking his teeth over his lower lip.

Qaed let out a sound akin to a whine, pressing himself against Clement's knee. "Whatever you want," he managed.

A teasing smile tugged at Clement's lips. "Be more specific." He'd gotten bold since his first time with Qaed–mainly because he knew it drove Qaed mad. Qaed liked a bit of a challenge.

Qaed captured Clement's jaw in his hand, pulling him in for a kiss that was all teeth and tongue. "I am going to fill every pretty little hole of yours," he managed between hot, open-mouthed kisses. "Do you want that? Do you want to be filled by me, my Clement?"

My Clement. He liked the sound of that. "Yes," he whimpered, every ounce of bravado draining from him. He couldn't help it. He was putty in this man's hands, no matter what he did.

"Yes, what?"

God, Clement was going to combust. "Yes, *sir.*"

"Good boy." He coaxed Clement's t-shirt from his body and kissed down his torso with reverence; trailing his mouth over his nipples, down his soft stomach that spilled over the waistband of his sweatpants. Qaed hooked his thick fingers into it and pulled his pants and boxer briefs down, and he sucked in a breath like he'd never seen this part of Clement before.

Clement helped kick his pants off, his hips already moving up against nothing in wanton anticipation. He was no stranger to what was to come; this man was damn good with his tongue.

And he was all too eager to remind Clement of that. His tongue swirled around Clement's engorged cock, and Clement's fists immediately found the comforter beneath him. "Fuck, Qaed," he bit out, thighs coming up to bracket Qaed's body.

He answered by hoisting Clement's thick thighs over his shoulders, forcing Clement open wider. He pointed his tongue inside Clement, and Clement immediately reached for Qaed's horns, giving them the sharp tug that he already knew would draw a reaction from him.

And it did. Qaed's moan vibrated against Clement, and Clement's hips snapped up against Qaed's face. He hardly recognized the sounds spilling from his own lips; some of it was Qaed's name, some of it desperate pleas for more. More of what, he didn't even know. He just needed *Qaed*.

"I want you inside me, Qaed," he breathed, giving his horn another experimental tug. Qaed's fingers dug deeper into his thighs in response. "Please."

"Have some patience. I do not want to hurt you," Qaed murmured, but *God,* did Clement want Qaed to hurt him. He wanted to feel Qaed with every step he took tomorrow and for the next week. He wanted to be absolutely wrecked. Qaed pressed loving kisses to the inside of Clement's thighs before lowering him back to the bed.

He retrieved a bottle of lube from his bedside table and covered one of his thick fingers with it. Clement squeezed his thighs together in anticipation. He had yet to feel Qaed inside him in his entirety, and frankly, he wasn't entirely sure his body could handle it. But he was love-drunk enough to want to try.

Qaed pressed a finger into his puckered entrance slowly, the unfamiliar sensation causing Clement to wince. Qaed's finger was already double the width of a human finger, which didn't exactly allow him to ease into the sensation. But he moved his thumb to circle Clement's cock, which proved a hell of a distraction.

"Shit," Clement gasped, clutching the wrist of the hand Qaed was steadying himself with. Just as the burn started to give way to comfort, Qaed slipped another finger in. Clement cried out against the sensation, and Qaed shifted his hand slightly to hold Clement's. To ground him.

"You are doing so well, love," Qaed murmured, leaning down to press a kiss to Clement's sternum. "Are you alright?"

Clement was *more* than alright. Hell, if he could live the rest of his life with every one of Qaed's fingers on him at all times, he would. "Yes," he managed, pushing his hips into Qaed's hand. "Qaed, I'm ready for you. Please."

"I will go slow," Qaed promised, and Clement wanted to shake him for being so fucking polite.

He was going to have to turn things up a notch. He dragged Qaed to his level by the horn. "Please, sir, *don't* go slow," he said raggedly into the join of Qaed's neck and shoulder, the very spot he knew would send him into a frenzy.

And he was right. "If you keep talking to me like that, I will not be able to control myself."

"Good." Clement sunk his teeth into that sensitive spot then soothed the bite with his tongue. Qaed let out a moan that he attempted to muffle by drawing his lips in between his teeth. But Clement knew the effect he had on him. "I want you to absolutely ruin me. *Sir.*"

And Clement got his wish. Qaed removed his fingers from Clement and he didn't have the time to lament the feeling of them before Qaed slammed into him. His lower dick pistoned in and out of the hole Qaed had just been lavishing with his tongue, his upper dick slapping lewdly against Clement's stomach. The sight in itself was nearly enough to drive Clement over the edge.

The hard ridges of Qaed's cock rubbed against Clement's with each thrust. "Yes, Qaed, *fuck* that's so good," Clement whined, pressing himself into Qaed. But yet, his body hungered for more. He captured Qaed's free erection in his hand and brushed his thumb over his leaking slit. Qaed's voice cracked as he moaned, steadying himself with a hand on Clement's chest.

"Are you ready for more?" Qaed asked.

Clement wasn't entirely sure, but he was going to try to be. "Yeah," he breathed, giving Qaed one long, slow stroke before releasing him. Qaed pulled out just long enough to shift his attention to Clement's forgotten, stretched hole that was begging to be filled. He pushed both cocks into Clement at the same time, engulfing the entire lower half of his body in flames.

Adjusting to Qaed again in his already abused hole was easy, but the sensation of his ass being filled to the brim with Qaed was foreign, verging on painful. He let out a series of whimpers of both pain and pleasure, and Qaed soothed him with a stroke of his hand over his sweat-soaked hair. "Gods, look at you. Taking all of me like you were born to do it." He trailed his thumb over Clement's lips and his tongue darted out to capture it. If he was going to be full of Qaed, his mouth might as well be as well.

He didn't move until Clement started to press his hips up against him, and he took that as an invitation to truly rip Clement apart. He fucked into Clement until he was seeing stars, Clement's fists balling into the comforter to ground himself.

Qaed's hand shifted down to the base of Clement's throat, not putting forth much pressure but *God,* was it hot.

Clement's orgasm crested inside him, and he clenched his thighs around Qaed's hips, melding the two of them together so Clement couldn't tell where he ended and Qaed began. "I'm–Qaed," he breathed, clutching Qaed's wrist.

"What is it, Clement? Use your words," Qaed commanded, his voice low, husky. He was close too.

"Sir... I'm gonna come." The hand around Clement's throat tightened slightly as Clement came, his arousal spilling around Qaed's cocks. Qaed followed only moments later, filling Clement with ropes of hot cum.

An empty ache replaced the burn in the pit of Clement's stomach as Qaed pulled out of him and fell to his side, gasping for breath. Clement rolled onto his side, resting a hand on Qaed's chest. "How's your heart doing, old timer?" he teased breathlessly, pressing a kiss to the underside of his jaw.

"It seems that I am still alive. But honestly, if this is what takes me to an early grave, I would not be happier." He grinned, pulling Clement into his arms. Clement nestled his head under Qaed's chin. "Are *you* alright?"

The soreness was already starting to set in, but he didn't care. He was happy, deliriously so. He kissed Qaed's shoulder. "Never better."

Epilogue

Clement

Two Months Later

Clement didn't know why he'd ever wanted to stay on Earth. Everything Kratos had to offer was so much more beautiful, so much more exciting–and Alqen was no exception.

It was so incredibly different from Veterok-III. Qaed had mentioned its beauty in passing, but his words hadn't done the planet justice. Alqen was a planet made of aetherite, Qaed had called it; a mineral that reflected the sun's rays and made the entirety of the planet almost unbearably bright. Now Clement understood why Qaed couldn't see in the dark.

They were in the Twelfth Ward, Qaed said, a ward not far from where Qaed grew up. A ward filled to the brim with merchants and craftsmen, they'd arrived on the day of the ward's biggest market of the year. Qaed had been practically bursting at the seams the entire shuttle ride over.

The market appeared to be a permanent fixture; vendors were shielded from the sun reflecting off the planet's glass-like surface by large, half dome-shaped steel housings. Some of the vendors were out in the open, selling jewelry that glinted in the sun.

And the *smell*. If Clement wasn't hungry before, he definitely was now. The smoky aroma of charred vegetables and spices wafted through the air, and Clement's stomach growled in response. "This is so cool," he breathed, shifting closer to Qaed as he wrapped an arm around his shoulders.

"I never got to come as a child," Qaed said as they started their stroll down the bustling street. "So if you see me spending an irresponsible amount of money... no you do not."

Clement grinned. "Hey, you should. We have a lot to celebrate." He mashed his cheek against Qaed's shoulder. "I still can't believe you're leaving *tomorrow.*"

"Me either." Qaed turned his head to press a kiss to the top of Clement's. "Tell me it is too late to change my mind."

"You're going, dummy." Clement stopped, forcing Qaed to stop as well. "You worked so hard for this. And you're gonna be great." He captured Qaed's lips in a kiss, blinking back the tears prickling behind his eyelids. He'd had plenty of time to sit with Qaed's inevitable departure. He'd only be with the wrestlers for a few months, but to Clement, that sounded like an eternity.

"And you are going to finish your edits and when I come back, we will have a lot of celebrating to do," Qaed murmured against Clement's lips. His edits. Because he was an *agented* author now. Kora had been enthusiastic about the whole thing, promising Clement there wasn't much editing to do. But that had done little to ease his nerves.

"We're in public. Don't talk about celebrating," Clement whispered, giving Qaed's chest a teasing smack.

A throat cleared behind them, and Clement sprang out of Qaed's arms. A qintaril a full half foot taller than Qaed and double his width stood behind them, arms folded over his chest. "Surely you two get enough action at home without having to kiss in the middle of the bazaar, too?"

Qaed huffed, giving the other qintaril a shove. He said something in his native language, eliciting a barked laugh from the stranger. "Clement, this is Vendi. Please forgive his rudeness."

Clement had heard about Vendi in passing and occasionally from Candy. The one thing she'd said about him was that he was massive and *very* hot, both of which proved to be true. He looked like a giant version of Votra, bearing the same deep blue skin and bone-colored horns. But his biceps were as big around as Clement's head.

"Oh, no, it's okay, *we* were being rude," Clement said quickly, holding his hands up in surrender. "I-I'm Clement."

Vendi grinned, and Clement was starting to see the resemblance between her and Qaed. "I know. Believe me, Qaed never stops talking about you," Vendi said. Clement flushed. "Shall we get some food?"

They continued their walk down the street, Clement's arm looped around Qaed's. "How long are you on Alqen?" Qaed asked, taking a pause at a stall with shimmering jewels on display. Clement's eyes grew wide. He'd never been much of a jewelry guy, but the gems displayed on the table in front of him were unlike any he'd ever seen. Many of them were clear stones almost resembling diamonds, inlaid in rings, bracelets, dangling from golden chains. But a silver ring bearing a glittering stone the color of honey caught Clement's eye.

"A while, most likely." Vendi hung out at the edge of the booth, not quite as taken with the jewelry as Qaed and Clement. "I am taking a bit of a break... possibly to take on a slightly less strenuous job."

Qaed scoffed but edged closer to Clement, peering down at the ring in his hand. Clement didn't know what qintaril culture was like in regards to relationships—and even if they were similar to humans, they'd only been officially together for two months. He had *no* right to be looking at rings.

"A break? You? Are you ill?" Qaed asked, holding his hand out for the ring. Clement placed it in his palm and Qaed lifted it to the sun. It cast tiny shards of rainbow across the shaded booth, and Clement's mouth dropped open. Earth didn't have anything like this.

"No. Just not trying to end up in an early retirement." Vendi cleared her throat. "Not that there is anything wrong with that, of course—"

"Good. I am glad to see you looking out for yourself," Qaed said simply. If he was bothered by her words, he did a good job of not showing it. But he returned the ring to Clement and smiled. Genuinely smiled. Clement's heart clenched, and he returned the ring to its display with a quick 'thank you' towards the vendor.

"I have a feeling I will be stuck here for a while. It is quite difficult to find simpler jobs," Vendi said, and Clement forced himself away from the table so as not to let himself get too attached to the ring.

Luckily, Vendi was proving to be a good distraction. "I might have a lead for you," he said. "My sister's friend needs a bodyguard for her galactic tour. She had a fan break into her hotel room back on Earth so her manager's bumping up her security."

Vendi's brow lifted. "A bodyguard for a... pop star?"

Well, Darby wasn't exactly a *pop* star. Clement had been a fan of hers for years and had practically choked when Cecily told him she'd not only met her, but become her friend. It wasn't shocking for Cecily, though. She could befriend a particularly friendly-shaped rock.

Qaed joined them after a moment, stuffing his hands into the pockets of his baggy black pants. "That would be good for you, Vendi," he said. "Maybe you two can talk about it while I go and get something."

Clement raised his eyebrows. "Get something?"

"Yes. I will be right back." He leaned in and brushed his lips across Clement's cheek before practically jogging deeper into the market. *Weird.* Clement stared after him for a second, his thoughts interrupted by a sharp laugh from Vendi.

"He has not learned how to be more subtle, has he?" she asked.

"Nope." Clement forced his eyes away from Qaed's receding form and back up to Vendi. "You don't have to take the bodyguard job, by the way. I'm not trying to, like, force you into it or anything–"

"No, it might be good for me." Vendi sighed, jerking her head toward a set of benches on the opposite side of the street. It was only then that he noticed her favoring one of her legs. He followed her and pretended not to notice how much she struggled to sit. "Tell me about this friend."

Clement draped an arm over the back of the bench. "Well, she's not exactly a *pop star*. She's more of, like... a spooky witch who sings songs to lure men into her swamp and eat them." Vendi blinked at him. Okay, so her sense of humor was certainly not the same as Qaed's. "Uh, she's a singer, and, like I said, she had some kind of scary things happen during her Earth tour so her management's making her get a bodyguard for her Kratos tour. The job would be pretty short. I think she has stops on every planet in Kratos, but it's only, like, twenty shows?" Vendi made a noncommittal sound. "Anyway, Cecily wanted me to see if I knew someone that I could trust to keep Darby safe. And I figure... if Qaed trusts you, then so do I."

Vendi's face was unreadable–the Vendi that existed without Qaed around was *very* different. "I will think about it," he said finally. "Can I give you an answer in a few days?"

"Sure!" Clement tapped his comm to Vendi's, still not entirely sure if this exchange had been successful or not. "Thanks, Vendi."

"I should be the one thanking you." Vendi wedged his hands between his knees, his gaze focused straight ahead. "Qaed has been much more open lately, more than he has ever been before. He kept a lot of secrets from Votra and I, but ever since you have been around, he has not been quite so closed off."

Don't cry. You can't cry in front of Vendi. Clement swallowed back the lump forming at the back of his throat. "It took a while. He *really* doesn't like to talk about himself, huh?"

"Not at all. But the three of us are one in the same." Vendi pushed herself off the bench with a grunt as Qaed rejoined them, the corners of his lips begging to pull into a smile. "Did you find what you were looking for?"

"Yes," Qaed said, his eyes meeting Clement's. "Shall we get some food?"

They continued through the market until Vendi forced them to stop at a stall selling some sort of vegetable in a spiced sauce, which Clement was slowly starting to learn was the epitome of Alqen food. They ate at a table a few feet from the stall, and Clement wasn't sure he could ever remember being this happy.

They said their goodbyes to Vendi after a few hours of roaming, a bit of impulse buying on Clement's part, and entirely too much food. He was more than ready to crawl into bed with Qaed once they returned home, maybe burn off some of these calories with sleepy yet enthusiastic sex.

"I really like Vendi," Clement said once they were back in the shuttle, stifling a yawn. "She's... a little scary. But nice."

"I promise she is nothing to be afraid of. It just takes time for her to trust people. But she likes you. I can tell." Qaed switched the shuttle on, the engine purring beneath them. "I am glad you got to meet her. It truly means the world to me."

Clement smiled, fighting back tears for far from the first time today. "And now, you have to meet Cecily. God help you."

"I will try my best to impress her," Qaed said, and Clement couldn't help but lift his brows. The lack of snarky comeback almost made him nervous.

"You doing okay there, bud?" Clement asked, pressing the back of his hand to Qaed's ever-cool forehead. "You're acting weird."

"Am I?" Qaed laughed, the sound forced. "I think I am acting perfectly normal."

"I've lived with you long enough to know that this is *not* your normal." Maybe he was just tired. They'd had a long day–they'd gone to the market immediately after the five-hour flight to Alqen, and they were about to brave the flight back so Qaed could leave for the Doletov district first thing in the morning. The poor man had to be dead on his feet.

Qaed finally gave in, letting out a sigh he must have been holding in for a while. "I wanted to do this right, Clem. I wanted to take you somewhere beautiful, somewhere... romantic. I wanted this to be something you would remember forever, but dammit, I do not know if I can wait another second longer."

Clement's heart jumped. "Qaed, what are you talking about?"

Qaed turned in his seat, digging through one of his pockets. "I did some research, and I learned that humans propose with rings."

No fucking way. There was no way this was happening. Clement's pulse rushed in his ears, and he unfastened his seatbelt. "Qaed–"

"But I also know that humans wait longer than qintaril do. We are of the opinion that our bodies know. I was created to find you. To know you. To love you." Qaed's voice grew thick, and Clement couldn't continue his battle against the tears anymore. "We do not have ceremonies like humans do. But we have a word. *Ta'qel.* The ones we choose to dedicate our lives to. And you are mine." He held out his hand, upon which sat a small metal cube that clasped in the front. "You do not have to make up your mind now. But I want to be clear about my feelings for you."

Clement had imagined being proposed to in many different ways. On a boat, at a fancy restaurant. Even in bed, whispered in the throes of passion. In the passenger seat of a shuttle wasn't one of those ways.

But maybe that was what made it so perfect. He had found someone who was so excited to be with him forever, he couldn't wait for the perfect moment. With trembling fingers, Clement opened the box. Inside it sat the ring he'd picked up at the booth. A tearful laugh bubbled from his lips and he slid it onto his ring finger.

This was perfect. He launched himself into Qaed's arms and kissed him with all of his might, the salt of his tears mingling with the kiss. "You wanna get human married to me?" he asked against Qaed's lips.

"If that is what you want... then yes," Qaed said, a hand resting at the nape of Clement's neck. "I would do anything for you, Clement Hall."

Clement pulled back just enough to give himself a clear view of Qaed's tear-filled eyes. "I wanna marry you," he whispered, his voice breaking under the weight of words he wasn't sure he'd ever say to anyone.

"Then we will make it happen." Qaed kissed away the tears streaking down Clement's cheeks, and all Clement wanted to do was stay in this exact moment forever.

Clement forced himself out of Qaed's arms, sniffing as he fastened his seat belt. "It was a real dick move to do this right before you're about to be on the opposite side of the planet from me for three months," he laughed, immediately claiming one of Qaed's hands and holding it in his lap.

"It kind of was, huh?" Qaed grinned, squeezing Clement's fingers as the shuttle took off. "I am sorry, Clement. I think I just... could not face the idea of leaving without telling you how I was feeling."

"Wow. Character development," Clement teased. "We love an emotionally available man."

"Alright, alright. Do not ruin the moment." But Qaed drew Clement's hand to his lips and kissed it, and Clement couldn't imagine being proposed to any other way.

"I do have *one* question, though." Clement turned to look at Qaed. "What did you have to get after we stopped at the ring place?"

Qaed cleared his throat. "I knew I could not be around you immediately after buying the ring, so I may have... just done a lap around the market."

God, Clement loved this man. "You really do like me, huh?"

"Something like that."

Acknowledgements

It still doesn't feel real to be writing a second set of acknowledgements, and I feel like I have even more people to thank this time.

As always, thank you to A.M. De la Rosa, my partner in crime, the person who everything I do is inspired by. Thank you for creating this world with me. Everyone, go check out Off Course, PLEASE. You won't regret it.

The biggest chunk of my thanks goes to the gay people in my phone, once again. Thank you to Noah for the invention of neverclear and being the reason Qaed lost his horn. Thank you to Elliot and Nicole, my earliest cheerleaders and critique partners. Thank you Lily for single-handedly fueling me with all of your Qaed thirst comments, I adore you. Thank you to Eliza for reading both Starcrossed and Stars Align early on, and always being the kindest person ever.

Thank you to jinku.pumpkin for once again delivering the most beautiful cover I could have imagined.

And thank you to my beta readers, Lyra, Melissa, Claire, and Rachel, for helping my book be the best it can be.

My biggest thanks, of course, goes to you. Thank you for reading this book.

www.ingramcontent.com/pod-product-compliance
Lightning Source LLC
Chambersburg PA
CBHW050403110726
47899CB00008B/2628